LOVE and WAR in BOSNIA

For the past undisclosed number of years, **Humayun Kabir** has thoroughly bucked the system. He lives in Kolkata, having spent most of his childhood in a remote village in West Midnapore in West Bengal. After completing his PhD, he joined in the State Civil Service and subsequently the Indian Police Service and served as the subdivisional police officer in several subdivisions. Afterwards, he served as the superintendent of police of several districts. His last role was as police commissioner of Chandannagar before he resigned and joined politics.

During his successful police career, Dr Kabir was an achiever, amassing a slew of impressive gruesome crimes solved, associated with controversy and political activities of the state.

Since childhood, he has been fond of writing short stories and has written a few novels in Bengali. *Love and War in Bosnia* is his first English-language fiction novel, based on his experiences as a part of the peacekeeping and restructuring force with the United Nations Mission in Bosnia and Herzegovina in the year 2001–02.

When he's not writing, he can be found reading the news, engaging in social service and enjoying meaningful conversations with friends.

LOVE and WAR in BOSNIA

Humayun Kabir

RUPA

Published by
Rupa Publications India Pvt. Ltd 2023
7/16, Ansari Road, Daryaganj
New Delhi 110002

Sales centres:
Allahabad Bengaluru Chennai
Hyderabad Jaipur Kathmandu
Calcutta Mumbai

Copyright © Humayun Kabir 2023

This is a work of fiction. Names, characters, places and incidents are either the product of the author's imagination or are used fictitiously and any resemblance to any actual person, living or dead, events or locales is entirely coincidental.

All rights reserved.

No part of this publication may be reproduced, transmitted, or stored in a retrieval system, in any form or by any means, electronic, mechanical, photocopying, recording or otherwise, without the prior permission of the publisher.

P-ISBN: 978-93-5702-004-6
E-ISBN: 978-93-5702-009-1

First impression 2023

10 9 8 7 6 5 4 3 2 1

The moral right of the author has been asserted.

Printed in India

This book is sold subject to the condition that it shall not, by way of trade or otherwise, be lent, resold, hired out, or otherwise circulated, without the publisher's prior consent, in any form of binding or cover other than that in which it is published.

*Dedicated to the innocent Bosnian
lives lost in the fray.*

One

'This weariness forgive me oh my Lord, if ever on my way I do fall back.' With these words, Rabindranath Tagore, at the age of fifty-three, documented his fatigue while sitting in Santiniketan in the month of Durga Puja. In these lyrics set to Taal Dadra and Imon-Kalyan, the poet not only notes the tiredness he felt but also apologizes for the frailty, failures and the lack in him. Fame does not guarantee the absence of indolence. Swami Vivekananda's exhaustion and melancholy can be heard in a speech he made a few days before he left his mortal coil. James Bond's enervation became evident when he jumped into the sea from a skyscraper. Madhubala, too, grew tired of hearing praises of her exquisite beauty. The average people soon tire of the fake promises of their puckish leaders. From Tagore to the *aam aadmi* (common man), fatigue is alien to none. Exhaustion is, therefore, a universal phenomenon.

Who am I? I am Sabyasachi, a mid-ranking police officer. That makes me an officer working on the ground. Though not on the battlefield, I work in the alleys, in the hills, in the woods, on the streets, in the den of criminals, or in the cushy yet cold house of white-collar criminals. Murder, kidnapping, robbery, burglary, cheating, rape, seduction—thrilling crimes and felony galore.

Cop! Old friends all avoid me unless they are in a crisis. There is something to be said about the inherent policeman in all of us, waiting to jump out when confronted with injustice. Add to that the might of the government machinery, a pistol at the waist and a stick in the hand, and the adrenaline keeps pumping. Despite being trained in this manner as a policeman, I was knackered a few years into the job.

It was the middle of the third week of June in 2001. A few days ago, in the context of a police operation in Salt Lake Stadium Complex, Calcutta and the surrounding areas, under my leadership, something had happened in the darkness of the night, which dragged me into a nasty political debacle. I was brought down by unbridled criticism and unchecked rumours, in spite of having honestly performed my duties. I was presented as a villain, demoralizing me and almost forcing me into hiding. Though I tried to console myself, reciting various encouraging verses, the fatigue was too strong to defeat.

Under such a humiliated state of my mind, I was presented with the opportunity of going to Bosnia and Herzegovina as a representative of my country on behalf of the United Nations (UN). All I knew about Bosnia-Herzegovina was from a faint memory of a history lesson about the biggest civil war since World War II in south-eastern Europe on Yugoslav soil in 1992. It was the same year that the Olympics was hosted by Barcelona, the year Bill Clinton defeated George H.W. Bush in the US presidential race and the *kar sevak*s (religious volunteers) demolished the Babri Masjid in India. Mani Ratnam's *Roja* shook the country, and Shah Rukh Khan's Raju became a gentleman. By the time the Bosnian War ended in 1995, *Dilwale Dulhania Le Jayenge* was ruling the box office and the prime minister of Israel, Yitzhak Rabin, had been assassinated. Casualties of the war were reported to be one-fifth of a million, with two million left homeless. The Socialist Federal Republic of Yugoslavia was completely annihilated in the civil war, broken up into pieces.

Everything that has a beginning must have an end, and the war, too, ended in November 1995. The Dayton Agreement was signed in December, but the damage from the war had left the region shattered—everything, from the economy to the social system, was in a shambles. Necessitated by this destruction, the Dayton Agreement called for international representatives from around the world—including India—to ensure peace during the reconstruction of Bosnia and Herzegovina.

This kind of work can be one of the most fulfilling experiences of a serviceman's life and so I jumped out of my chair when the opportunity presented itself. I was also motivated by the experiences narrated by two members of the West Bengal cadre who had recently returned from Bosnia. It seemed that if one could tolerate the chilling winter, ignore the warm proximity of the *urvashi*s (beautiful girls) dancing in the bars and nightclubs and overcome the fear of insurgent hostility, one was rewarded with all the benefits that come with the living and travelling in Europe, including the tax-free ₹1.5 million. Disillusioned with and exhausted by my work in the previous years, my mind sought adventure—the decision was easy.

Before Puja, I received a letter from the Ministry of Home Affairs in Delhi, directing me to report to the Indo-Tibetan Border Police (ITBP) headquarters to appear for a test. As soon as Puja duty was over, I left for Delhi. Upon reaching the headquarter, I saw a huge crowd of 850-odd aspiring candidates for a meagre fifty seats. *Gosh, Goodness! It's a very tough competition, nerve-wracking matter!*

Being an innocent village lad, the inherent and deep-rooted inferiority complex in my subconscious always makes me feel subdued—a fear of competition deeply rooted in me. Frankly speaking, I was supposedly a 'bit stupid' since childhood, an adjective I have often heard my parents, neighbours and teachers use to describe me. My childhood friend, Pratima Gayen, used to slap me on the head every now and then, saying, 'You big fool!' Woodpeckers and bumblebees had made the Arjuna tree under the thatched roof of our mud house their abode. Black, jumbo-sized insects would hover around my face—like a helicopter—whispering in my ear, as if to say, 'You stupid fool'. I accepted their verdict on my intelligence. The first boy in our class, Govinda Jana, used to tell me that if you apply less or no mustard oil on your head, you will become more intelligent! But my mother would not listen, she would say, 'Stupid! Govinda may be securing first place in class, but he doesn't know anything. Mustard oil on the head will help you withstand cold and the schoolmaster will not be able to pull your hair time and again, as it will slip. It helps expand your intellect, not supress it!'

Even after being in the police force for so long, the insecurities stayed. My mind started to wonder how I would match up to all these geniuses. People say that the police service is one where you do not need any knowledge, it is just about running after thieves. Knowledge and intellect are lost, or what is called '*dimag ki aisi ki taisi*'. Physical sciences, biology, history, geography, arithmetic, trigonometry, etc., are replaced with the Indian Penal Code and the Criminal Procedure Code, with various complex legal manipulations and applied politics, commonly known as 'tact'. Crisis management and the ability to manage situations by hook or by crook!

We were told during the briefing that out of fifty seats, fifteen were in Bosnia and thirty-five in Kosovo. A range of tests would be conducted, evaluating different competencies. English language skills would be tested with video and audio tapes played in different accents. Once the tapes are over, answers are to be recorded on a sheet, with a final interview round conducted completely in English. Other tests included driving skills and firearm shooting skills. Of course, I have no problem shooting a gun. The tests would continue for four days in the presence of examiners from the UN, representing the US, Ireland, Ghana and Argentina.

Members from every unit were present—CBI, BSF, CRPF,

ITBP, SIB. Members of one unit would be looking down on the members of another unit, doubting their capabilities of carrying out a UN mission. Candidates from the CBI believed themselves to be the top contenders—after all, when all the opponents rely on them for investigations, they should be given priority. But those like us who were in the police, who toil on the streets, day and night, for the safety and security of the public, how are we any less than the others? Don't we solve cases like James Bond within the time limit set by society, carrying the burden of worldly nuisance, tolerating the criticism and the sarcastic comments of newspaper correspondents and their editorials? But even among the police, the Delhi Police officers often look down on the Bengal Police officers, wondering how the latter is fit for a UN mission when all they know is how to play the harmonium.

The overall atmosphere of the room made me tense. It reminded me of the stress before an exam in school. The lengthy wait in the hall with others reminded me of my school life. My professional experience and knowledge may be good in the arena of politics, but years of police work had suppressed my academic intellect, like sediments in the Padma River.

All the waiting candidates crowded the officers who completed the test, inundating them with questions: 'What was the pattern?', 'What was asked?', 'How tough was it?' Those who had crossed the hurdle said with grim surety, 'Hey, brother, there is nothing like a pattern! Yes, there are some foreign altercations played in the tape recorder. You have to follow it minutely and write your answers accordingly.' An officer from Kerala passed a comment, 'Should they play the quarrel in Gurgaon-wala Hindi for your convenience instead of in a foreign language?'

As the exams of our batch began, I listened intently to the narrative of a tussle between four foreigners. Suddenly, a Madhya Pradesh police officer sitting beside me stood up and started shouting, '*Ajib musibbat hai, mujhe kuch samaj nahi aa raha hai* (I am in trouble! I can't understand anything).'

'*Aagle saal samaj lena, aabhi chup chaap baitho yaar* (Listen properly in the test next year, now sit down and remain silent).'

Some people around him almost forced Ajib Musibbat (strange trouble-maker) to sit down.

Somehow, I completed the test. The result was declared on the last day. Holding my breath, I checked the list of names from the bottom, browsing up to the top, and when I had nearly given up, I found my name—I was one step closer to my goal. For driving, I had heard that they were making drivers take the slalom test, where the candidates were asked to drive in reverse gear up to a garage, park the car only using the rear-view mirrors. I drove very cautiously, and with a little bit of luck, got through without any accidents. For the shooting test, I imagined the target to be a known criminal and fired thirty rounds on target, an absolute *bajimat* (triumph).

Back in Howrah, I received news that I had to report back in Delhi in the last week of November. The letter contained specific instructions to help candidates prepare for the move. We needed to carry winter clothes and at least four sets of uniform—navy-blue trousers with sky-blue shirts—stitched at the cantonment in Delhi. I contacted Siddhartha Sen, a history student who had been selected from the last batch but had not been able to go because of family reasons, who would be joining us this time. I am not of the view that colleagues can be considered friends, but Siddhartha was a colleague and a friend—a genuine one at that.

The options were to go to Bosnia or Kosovo to join the United Nations Peacekeeping Forces, or in other terms, the UN International Police Task Force (IPTF). I opted for Bosnia-Herzegovina.

Siddhartha was happy to hear that I was joining the Bosnia

team. He gave me a historical overview of the country and said, 'You were a science student, so you need not worry about memorizing history with your already-tired brain. I'll inject the history of Bosnia-Herzegovina into your subconscious mind just like vaccinating the subcutaneous layer of your skin, by narrating the history little by little, like a story.' I also did my own research and now knew the latitude and longitude of Bosnia and that it is a southeast European country, with an extension of the Alps and the Adriatic Sea coast running along the Neum corridor. I learnt about the weather, the food, the culture, the accommodation and, of course, the sociopolitical problems of the region.

Walking around Chandni Market with Siddhartha, we bought clothes, leather jackets and boots, etc., and waited for the green signal from the Ministry of Home Affairs. The fax arrived in the last week of November. Finally, I had achieved my goal. I was going to Bosnia! The problem now was that my luggage weighed 80 kilos. I had stuffed into my bags everything I could think of, from Govinda Bhog rice to moong dal, home-made ghee, a bottle of mixed pickle and coconut ladoos. Vegetables like potatoes, onion, garlic, ginger and carrots were to be taken from Delhi. But I was only allowed 60 kilos when leaving from Delhi, and would have to make the difficult decision of what to leave behind.

Arriving in Delhi, our uniforms were distributed, and ITBP started processing our official passports, visas, etc. We attended induction sessions and wandered around Connaught Place and Bengali Market. We bought a few more things and started to pack our bags. We knew we were going to a country where the situation was precarious and didn't want to be unprepared.

War-torn Sarajevo, the capital of Bosnia-Herzegovina, had a tendency to change colours—the situation could change in the blink of an eye, from green to amber or orange to red zone;

in fact, Bosnia-Herzegovina itself was completely a grey zone. In a moment, what appeared safe could turn dangerous. Such was its unpredictability.

Siddhartha reiterated our mission, 'We have been deputized to keep the situation under control, not just make sure it doesn't get worse but also aid in reconstruction. The UN is spending a lot of money to ensure rule of law is maintained in the region. Fighting in the name of ethnicity and religion has led to all kinds of heinous acts, from ethnic cleansing to dumping of hundreds of dead bodies in mass graves, for years together. Some of the incidents have been termed as genocide by the UN and the International Court of Justice. Our job is to help the country restructure, form laws, reconstruct constitutional provisions and help recover from the shock the devastation has caused its people.'

Ethnic cleansing! Killing people of other ethnicity in the name of religion or caste and creed; this killing in the name of an imaginary entity has brought the Earth to the brink of extinction. Even though we know that the observance of religion is gratuitous, not just when alive but even after death, which reiterates that it is nothing but a big farce. The bubble of this farce bursts when we burn the mortal body or bury it six feet under the ground. Does anyone know where their beloved one has gone, the road to heaven or the stairs of hell? There is not a single instance in the world where religion has been of use to mankind. In India, many people incite religious groups for the sake of politics. Violence in the name of religion might destroy the world faster than global warming!

Siddhartha argued that, 'Religion promotes peace of mind and concentration. It helps people unite!' But uniting by unknowingly creating an opponent is the most dangerous thing. If there is no religion, the tunes of all the people could be harmonized, *mile sur mera tumhara, toh sur bane hamara* (our tunes are connected, yours and mine)—the river of melodies of harmony would overflow all around.

As a wholehearted religious person, Siddhartha declared a ceasefire in the argument about *religion* and said, 'You have caught a cold again. Let me take you to a doctor tomorrow. We will have to take some medicine as prophylactic. You know, five months of the year, it snows in Bosnia.'

We had a few days to ourselves before we had to leave, and I wanted to make the most of the time I had left in my country. We spent our mornings on the streets of Old Delhi, which kept beckoning us with the history written in its lanes and bylanes—the eventful era of Mughal India. Siddhartha, who spent a few years in Delhi in his early life, now acted as a philosopher and guide showing me around.

And then the diplomatic passports were ready and it was time to go. We were to leave on 25/26 December midnight. We had a layover at Zurich, from where Sarajevo is only a two-hour flight. My heart danced with joy and I planned on making the most out of the four hours we were getting in Zurich. It was my dream city, after all!

When the day arrived, everything went by smoothly and we boarded on time. Before the plane took off, Siddhartha took out a small dried flower from his chest pocket and touched it to his forehead before putting it back. Looking at me and realizing that I had caught him in the act, he grinned. I shrugged and said, 'Don't you consider yourself a progressive person? Superstition, like faith on a deity's flower, doesn't suit you.'

Siddhartha mumbled, 'No, but my daughter is still quite young, you know?'

My friend's mind was heavy, he wasn't just leaving home, he was also going away from his little girl.

I looked out the window. The aircraft was still flying through the skies of Delhi. Both of us were fascinated watching the chain of light of Delhi. Slowly, the aircraft rose to an altitude of about 40,000 feet. The constant humming of the aircraft annoyed me, but soon, both of us fell asleep while we flew across the world towards new things.

Two

Following the announcement of the air crew, we set our watches to the international time. After a few turns around the airport, the aircraft headed towards the tarmac. Leaning forward, I tied my shoelaces and looked out the window. The view was bleak under the cloudy sky. At half past six, our aircraft landed in Zurich. Everyone disembarked. Queries revealed that our luggage could directly be collected from the Sarajevo airport, on arrival. Once the various immigration formalities were taken care of, we went straight to the executive lounge booked for us. There were four long hours before the connection. An officer of the Tamil Nadu IPS cadre was nominated to be our group commander, based on seniority. He instructed us to remain within the vicinity of the airport. There wasn't enough time to tour the city. Even within the Zurich airport, we were fascinated by the splendour of our surroundings and the people.

We entered the washroom to freshen up and were immediately taken by the cleanliness and ambience inside. As soon as I came out, Siddhartha said with a smirk, 'Didn't you fall asleep in the toilet?' I ignored his sarcasm and enquired about our next meal. I was famished after the long journey.

We were greeted by a generous spread on the dining table. After wolfing down cookies, burgers and cakes, I settled on the sofa with a glass of strawberry juice in my hand. No one was particularly engaged in the lounge. The sofa sets were scattered around the space and only a handful of people were seated. I looked outside through the glass pane while taking a sip of the fruit juice. It was about eight o'clock. A few fluorescent jackets were visible, shifting luggage onto carriages.

It grew darker outside, and a light breeze started blowing. Before I could enquire about the lack of visibility, white flakes floated in the air. Siddhartha shouted, 'Snowfall.'

Bengalis are rarely fortunate enough to witness snowfall on trips to hill stations like Darjeeling and Mussoorie. On the few occasions that we might experience this wonderful phenomenon, we cannot refrain from talking about it tirelessly.

I opened the glass door and stepped out onto the terrace. The gust of cold air and the fluttering snowflakes caressed my face. Fascinated, I spread my arms out and just then, I noticed a European couple smiling at me from inside the lounge. Ignoring them, I turned around and touched the light flakes with my hands and watched them melt on my fingers. Gradually, the wind picked up and the snow came down in swirling torrents. Siddhartha came out to fetch me. He reminded me that we still had to suffer through the frozen winter at Sarajevo. I shook off the snowflakes from my shoulder and pushed back into the lounge.

Growing up in a village, I moved to Calcutta for higher studies. After finishing my studies, I stayed on in the city for work. Although the headquarter was in Writers Building, I was frequently posted at different districts. I always preferred the ones closest to the mountains. During holidays, I would visit hill stations. But this was my first experience of snowfall. So, I sat on the sofa and continued to watch the snowfall, mesmerized.

I had slept fitfully on the flight, so I felt a bit drowsy. To overcome it, I decided to take a stroll. I grabbed my passport bag and went out to explore the departure lounge. There were hardly any people in that huge airport. The ground staff with their walkie-talkies and the occasional couples clad in designer clothes were the only people I chanced upon, the staccato sound of their heels echoing in the quiet of the night-time airport.

After about an hour, I returned to the lounge.

Our team leader informed us that the flight had been delayed due to bad weather in Sarajevo. So, finishing the rest of my strawberry juice, I eased myself on the sofa, eager to catch an hour of sleep. But that restful oblivion was hard to come by, as my mind kept wandering to Bosnia and its people. After a bit, I got up and decided to read the ITBP book on Bosnia instead. A copy had been handed to each of us as preparatory measures.

Eventually, it was announced that Sarajevo's weather had improved and our flight had been scheduled. Bag in hand, I followed the others to our flight. Peeping out the window, I noticed that my seat was near the wings of the small aircraft. Snow dust on the wings and the distant cloudy sky were my travelling companions. Our flight was delayed by a couple of hours.

The plane took off from Zurich airport and flew into the distant sky. The snowfall had stopped a while ago. Now the sun was radiant. We were flying at a low altitude. The snow-capped Alps unfurled below us, with the countless lakes in the city of Zurich reflecting the tranquillity of the sky. The scenic beauty of the terrain below and the brilliance of the sky above us were astounding. Four cabin crew served lunch to us on this short flight. The lunch menu was brief: a small bun, a stick of butter, some raw salad with marinated shrimps in a plastic bowl, and a little custard in a small plastic container. Ranga Swamy Rangarajan of Karnataka, seated near me, mumbled, 'I am a vegetarian.'

Immediately, a cabin crew grabbed the shrimp packet from his tray. Rangarajan asked for another custard box. But the thick accent and expressionless face of the lady towering over him was too intimidating for Rangarajan. He quietly picked up the bun, buttered it and proceeded to stuff it into his mouth. I felt sorry for him.

It is difficult to keep time on a flight. Before I knew it, two and a quarter hour had passed. With the 'fasten-the-seat belt' announcement, I came back to my senses. Looking down, I glimpsed the town of Sarajevo in the middle of the snow-capped Balkan Hills. It was a small town, marked by towering buildings, standing like sentinels amidst the frigid landscape. Thinking about the people of that war-torn country made my chest constrict. For the first time, the reality of my presence there hit me. To my surprise, I was only awash with compassion for the people who had died defending their independence and those who had been left behind in the aftermath. As the plane landed with a slight jolt, I realized that I had touched the ground of the accursed country. A cold white landscape greeted us on all sides as far as our eyes could see. Standing in the snow, I started sweating. When the group commander shouted, 'Hurry up, brothers!' I followed.

The small airport had no conveyor belts. Our suitcases were unloaded from the belly of the aircraft in a trolley. Completing the immigration formalities, I put my suitcase on the trolley. The cold gripped me like a numbing vice. Trembling, I pulled out the leather jacket from my suitcase and put it on. We had been told, repeatedly, that by 26 December, bone-chilling winter would have set in in Bosnia. But preoccupied with the plight of the people there, the warning had completely slipped out of my mind.

A long bus from the UN office was waiting for us outside the airport. An American police officer working at the UN local office came forward, 'Welcome to Sarajevo, welcome to the United Nations Mission in Bosnia and Herzegovina—UNMIBH,' he said. He took a list out of his pocket and matching our names against it, reported our arrival on his walkie-talkie to the Mission Headquarters (MHQ).

On seeing us, the bus driver came forward. Unlocking the

luggage carrier of the bus, he said in broken English, 'Put your luggage in there.' The bus left as soon as we boarded. The road was paved with trees on both sides. But not a leaf could be seen. The bare, snow-covered branches greeted us with the promise of a frost-bound winter. Small snow-covered houses were scattered along the road. Staring at the mountains looming around us, the American officer, said, 'There are mass graves in the crevices of that mountain.' *Mass graves*! It chilled me to the very core. No wonder Bosnia was called the 'Land of Mass Graves'!

I turned away from the scene outside. The people on the bus were cursing and lamenting the cold. But nobody was bothered about the mass graves. The American officer said that it had been snowing since the last seven days. The bus soon arrived at the city centre and stopped in front of the huge building—the United Nations Headquarters. The cars in the parking lot looked like neat rows of small mounds of snow. Two or three Indian officers from the previous batch working at the MHQ came out to greet us. They took us to the counter at the personnel section. Within half an hour, we were presented with our UN ID cards. This would be the proof of our attachment to the UNMIBH for the rest of our time here. I went to the next counter, showed the ID and received $1,000, which was equivalent to 2,500 Bosnian Deutsche Marks (DM). Food and accommodation were all at our own expenses, so, the amount was given as an advance.

We poured into the bus as freshly appointed aids of the UN and were whisked to Ilidža, a township on the other side of Sarajevo, where hotel rooms had been booked for us. On landing, Sarajevo greeted us with the ambience of a Hollywood horror film. As the bus turned the corner to arrive at our hotel, the gloomy street seemed to descend further into darkness. At only half past five, evening had set in. Hotel Owaza housed the reception, dining and ballroom in a one-story building.

The rooms were in separate cottages. The American officer who had accompanied us from the airport helped us check in and informed us that for the next seven days, we would have to attend our training at the headquarters. We would then be dispatched all over the country to our respective posts. I went to my cottage to clean up.

The hotel room was cosy, with an attached bathroom. It was centrally heated, with a part of the wall inlaid with lead panelling. Boiling water ran through the pipe to keep the room warm. The heat from the lead plates radiated throughout the room. A thermometer mounted on the opposite wall indicated that the room temperature was fixed at 8 degrees Celsius.

Exhausted from the long journey, I decided to take a hot bath in the bathtub. Later, I lay down in bed and immediately fell asleep. I don't know for how long I slept. The sound of the intercom roused me from my jet-lagged slumber. Struggling out from under the thick blankets, I picked up the phone. The girl on the other end was saying something in the local language, but I had no way to understand her. I was groggy, unable to shake off my fatigue. As I lay in the comfort of the sheets, wondering whether I should get up to look into the reason behind the call, the intercom rang again. This time, it was from our group commander, 'Come to dinner. It will not be available after nine o'clock.'

The wall clock read half past eight. I was already late. I got out from under the blanket and sat on the bed; the room felt warmer than before. Glancing at the thermometer, I noticed that it had shot up to 18 degrees Celsius. Wearing a leather jacket, I walked out of my room into a drizzle of snow. Wading through 6 inches of snow, I crossed the open road and the garden to reach the dining hall.

I picked up the menu card from the table, but it was written in Bosnian. Perplexed, I looked up to see Rangarajan smiling at me. He asked, 'May I help?'

'Yes, of course. But I would prefer non-veg,' I said.

His face fell and he said, 'Then you better ask the others.' The food that I ordered after much deliberation was brought in about 10 minutes later by a beautiful young Bosnian lady. She laid down a small bowl of boiled cabbages, with a very thick rice soup, a fried fish and a small bowl containing crushed garlic dipped in olive oil. She smiled sweetly and said, '*Dobre Viche*.' It seemed like a greeting, so I smiled and nodded at her. The next day, I learned that *Dobre Viche* meant 'Good Afternoon' or 'Good Evening'.

The fish looked like our big bata or mrigel pona. The food was bland. I used salt and tomato ketchup from the table to somehow swallow my dinner. On our way back from the dining hall, one of my colleagues muttered, 'These people don't know the use of spices.'

Three

Classes commenced at 10 a.m. on 26 December at the MHQ. The first class was on Bosnian history. An American woman named Sandra Furnary was our teacher. We had already been given several books on that subject. On a map, I found the Adriatic Sea to the east of Italy, and we were sitting in a classroom on its eastern shores in Bosnia-Herzegovina. Sarajevo was closer to Rome than Milan. Bosnia was about one-fourth the size of Switzerland or slightly smaller than Himachal Pradesh. It was sparsely populated.

The introductory session ended with Sandra revealing her past and subsequent love for history. Our sixty-five-year-old teacher was born in a village near Philadelphia. She studied history at Harvard University. After working for a variety of organizations and teaching at Harvard for several years, she joined the UN. For the past five years, she had been touring various cities in Eastern Europe. Sandra preferred the stories hidden behind the prosaic pages of history books instead of dry facts. She made our lessons rather interesting in the process of narrating the history of Yugoslavia. She insisted on being called Sandra, without any honorifics, and identified herself as 'A student of history'.

Bosnia had both a bloody and a peaceful history of being occupied, starting from the Roman Empire, Byzantines, Slavs, Hungarians and Turks. In 1389, the Serbs lost to the Ottoman Turks at the Battle of Great Kosovo. In 1483, Bosnia surrendered to the Ottoman Turks, and Islam came inevitably with the mighty Ottoman army. This was a time of mass conversion from Christianity to Islam in Yugoslavia. The Ottoman Empire ruled over Bosnia for more than 400 years. Bosnia-Herzegovina was then essentially made up of three ethnic groups: 50 per cent Muslim, 31 per cent Serb (Orthodox Christian), 16 per cent Croat (Roman Catholic) and a small number of Jews. The origin of all of them was the Slovak race.

Finally, in the eighteenth century, the Ottoman Empire, weakened by civil war and internal strife, fell into the hands of the great European powers. Austria and Hungary, with external help from Russia, won against the Turks. Austria or Hungary could not decide who would take the lion's share of the war benefit, so the erstwhile Ottoman Empire remained scattered in the region until World War I.

I looked out the window of the conference hall. The evening was descending with the incessant snow. After our history class, we trickled out into the lobby. At the reception, a huge and tall Croatian beauty informed us that our bus would be delayed. The roads to our hotel had been snowed in. We were asked to wait in the canteen.

We were greeted by the bright smiles and *'Dobre Viche'* from several beautiful young women there. The food was laid out in glass cases. We sat down at the table with our cakes, sandwiches and hot coffee.

About 45 minutes later, our bus driver approached us. The bus was ready to take us back to our hotel, as the roads had been cleared out.

En route to our hotel, two escort vans started accompanying our bus. On enquiry, we learnt that the area had been placed under alert. So, the American Stabilizing Force was escorting us to safety. It was getting dark outside. We sat inside the bus, excitement and trepidation warring within. But we reached Hotel Owaza without incident.

Arriving at the hotel room, I rushed to freshen up before

dinner. Arriving at the dining hall, I found our team leader pacing. When the last of us arrived, he finally spoke, 'First thing in the morning, everyone needs to go to the MHQ and pick up the firearms issued to us. You are ordered to keep them close at all times for self-defence. This order has come directly from the MHQ.'

The new development left us rattled. Initially, I had thought that our main challenge would be adapting to the cold. In my naivety, I had assumed that we would be safe, at least for the seven days of training, and that any hostile situation would be faced only once we were posted in the operational area. We were informed that the bus would leave at nine o'clock next morning.

I woke up early next morning. But when I tried to open the door to my room, it wouldn't budge. I started assuming all kinds of nefarious intentions. But taming my irrational anxiety, I quickly pushed back the window curtains, hoping to find somebody outside to help me. I was greeted by a desolate white morning. Much like the sun, not a human soul was in sight. I left the window and came back to the bedside table, picked up the intercom receiver and called the reception. No one picked up. So, I called Siddhartha instead.

Siddhartha sounded excited on receiving my call. 'My door is also jammed shut due to snow. I have called the room service. They will come and remove the snow with pickaxe and shovel for our rescue.'

Meanwhile, the hands of the clock passed nine o'clock. By the time I reached the bus, it was half past ten.

Arriving at the MHQ, I learnt that Sandra had come searching for us twice. It was almost half past eleven when we arrived at our classroom with our firearms. Sandra was finally called on to enlighten our eager minds.

In the first decade of the twentieth century, the superpower Austria strangled the Bosnian separatists. Under pressure, the separatists decided to retaliate against the constant attacks and harassment. Desperate to teach Austria a lesson, 19-year-old Gavrilo Princip, a Serbian separatist from the Suicide Squad, recklessly shot and killed Austrian gem Archduke Franz Ferdinand on 28 June 1914 on a crowded street in Sarajevo.

History experts mark Ferdinand's assassination as the immediate cause of World War I. In the aftermath, many Muslims were fleeing Bosnia every day, spreading to other provinces of the Ottoman Empire. Surprisingly, the city of Sarajevo survived from the massacre of the war.

In 1917, World War I ended, leaving a pile of bodies in its wake. The Serbian rulers then formed Yugoslavia, assembling the Serbs, Slovenes and Croats. Due to their political proximity to the Austro-Hungarian rulers in the first half of the twentieth century, the Croats gradually gained strength. To cull their growing influence, a Serbian separatist group assassinated the Croatian leader Stjepan Radic at the Belgrade parliament in 1928. Parliament was dissolved and the Constitution was repealed. Amidst the changing map of Europe, Belgrade's military rulers tried to suppress all forms of rebellion. In collaboration with Italy, a separatist terrorist group called Ustaše was formed under the leadership of the Croatian lawyer and politician, Ante Pavelić. In 1934, they assassinated King Alexander of Yugoslavia during his trip to France. An era of chaos ensued. The global economic recession further complicated the sociopolitical turmoil in Yugoslavia. The Yugoslav Communist Party emerged in 1935–36 in the wake of this catastrophe.

In 1941, at the peak of World War II, Adolf Hitler invaded Yugoslavia. Slovenia was first taken over by the Nazi forces, and Croatia was occupied by fascist Italy. Bulgaria was rewarded with Macedonia for its loyalty to Germany. German puppet Milan Nedić came to power in Serbia. Pavelić, the leader of Ustaše, was engaged in ethnic cleansing. Orthodox Christian

Serbs were converting to Roman Catholicism to save their lives, and Muslims were identifying themselves as Muslim Croats. Meanwhile, General Nedić of the Royal Yugoslav Army shook hands with Germany. Germany rewarded Nedić. He became the prime minister of the Government of National Salvation. Nedić continued the extermination of non-Serbians, especially Jews. When the war ended, Yugoslav communists imprisoned him. Nedić jumped out of a prison window to his death in 1948.

In the midst of this anarchy, the formidable intelligence force of the Yugoslav Army, popularly known as the Chetniks, rose to power. They spread like wildfire in Serbia, Croatia and Bosnia, and counter-ethnic cleansing began. Now, the Croats and Muslims were targeted. Overnight, Bosnia turned into a butcher's shop.

The head of the Yugoslav Communist Party, Josip Broz Tito, stood strong against all separatist groups. One by one, the Nazi, Ustaše and Chetniks were all forced out. In 1945, Tito's party took over Yugoslavia.

After World War II, Marshal Tito severed all ties with Stalin and formed the Yugoslav National Army with western help. Under Marshal Tito's rule, the Christians and Muslims were not allowed to practise their religion openly, but cultural freedom prevailed for all. Eventually, Yugoslavia transformed into the Socialist Federal Republic of Yugoslavia (SFR Yugoslavia), a multi-ethnic republic, comprising Bosnia-Herzegovina, Serbia, Croatia, Slovenia, Montenegro and Macedonia. Marshal Tito died in 1980, and with him ended the short-lived peace in Yugoslavia.

In the 1960s, with the gradual decline of the communist ideology all over the world, Soviet Russia was also losing its control over Eastern Europe. After the Cold War, its effects on the SFR of Yugoslavia became apparent. In the absence of Marshal Tito, republics like Slovenia, Croatia, etc., rose to prominence.

Slobodan Milošević, the chairman of the Socialist Party, who became the president of the Serbian Republic in 1986, further accelerated the disintegration of the Yugoslavia (SFR). He lacked religious tolerance and dreamt of ethnic homogeneity in Serbia. He planned to repeal the federal constitution and establish a collective presidency in Yugoslavia. His famous speech on the 600th anniversary of the Great Kosovo War at the battlefield of Kosovo, on 26 June 1989, shook the foundation of Yugoslavia. While the Serbs rejoiced, the Muslims, the Croats and the Slovenians shuddered with fear.

In the 1990 election, the Communist Party remained only in Serbia and Montenegro. Parties that had been vocal about sovereignty of non-Serbians took over the rest of the republics. The same year, Milošević overthrew the autonomy of the Serb Minority Region, intervening in their education and politics. The non-Serbians, enraged by the intervention, retaliated.

Slovenia and Croatia declared independence on 25 June 1991. The Yugoslav National Army jumped at the behest of Milošević. In ten days, the Slovenes miserably defeated the Serbian National Army, dumped them in the Belgrade-bound train, stripping the soldiers down to their underwear. But Croatia had to pay a heavier price. Their fight against the Yugoslav National Army continued for six months. The worst hit were the Croatian port cities of Dubrovnik and Vukovar. The UN-negotiated ceasefire ended on a number of conditions. The independence of the two countries finally gained international recognition in January 1992.

Bosnia-Herzegovina declared its independence on 29 February 1992, amid anarchy in Eastern Europe. Serbs living in Bosnia demanded a separate state, and a fierce war broke out in April. On 5 April, Bosnian people took to the streets in Sarajevo to celebrate the independence of the Bosnian parliament. The joy soon turned to terror when the Yugoslav

National Army opened fire on the people. The army crossed the river Drina, entered Bosnia and clamped down on the Bosnians. It spread like wildfire from city to city, to the villages, turning the country into a mass grave.

The carnage that followed could well be compared to the horrors of World War II. Together, the Muslim-Croats were able to put up little resistance against the Yugoslav National Army and their collaborator nationalist Serbs. The genocide of Bosnian Muslim and Croat men, and the mass rape of women were a daily routine. One by one, people started fleeing their homes. The Serbian National Army burned village after village, with people trapped inside or sometimes empty houses. One by one, they blew up historic mosques, Catholic churches, synagogues, museums, libraries, offices, etc.

On 16 December 1992, the foreign ministers of the NATO countries unanimously agreed to send humanitarian aid to Bosnia and Herzegovina in support of UN resolutions. Although the US had agreed, Britain was reluctant to comment on the issue. On 25 December, US President George W. Bush threatened President Slobodan Milošević to stop expelling Albanians from Kosovo and ethnic cleansing, or he should be ready to face war. The UN had assigned its own protection force to ensure that no warship would fly over the air in Bosnia.

From the beginning of 1993, NATO started patrolling the air. In June of that year, they came forward to help the UN. In August, the North Atlantic Council decided to provide humanitarian assistance to the people of Bosnia and strike the Yugoslav National Army if necessary. After much warning, on 26 February 1994, with the permission of the UN, NATO and the US Air Force launched a joint attack on Serbian forces in Banja Luka. After that, the attack and counter-attack continued. Civilians were constantly being killed by the Yugoslav National Army in retaliation for the joint forces' attack on Serbian forces.

The NATO-led offensive aggression became intensified with the passage of time. The frustration of the Serbian army continued to grow along with the fatigue of long battles, the loss of life and the pressure of casualties.

Surrounded from all sides, the Serbian army abducted 364 UN peacekeepers and used them as human shields and bargaining chips. Failing to comply with the repeated requests, NATO and the US Air Force launched a series of coordinated attacks to rescue the UN peacekeepers on 25/26 May 1995, as well as destroyed Serbian weapons hoarded in Pale. In retaliation, the Serbian army attacked civilians in Sarajevo on 26 August. They fired indiscriminately at people on the streets and inside houses. There were countless casualties in that incident. This time, NATO and the Allied forces gave an ultimatum to the Serbian army to retreat. Without receiving any response, about 60 different types of warplanes launched simultaneous attacks on the Serbian forces. The Serbian army disintegrated due to the continued air strikes. Most of the Serbian soldiers escaped with their lives and melted in the melee. Ultimately, Bosnia-Herzegovina was occupied by the Allied powers; NATO and UN envoys got busy in establishing peace.

Meanwhile, on 4 June 1995, three of the worst conspirators of the twentieth century—Serbian Army Commander Colonel-General Ratko Mladić, Serb leader Radovan Karadžić and the head of the UN peacekeeping force from Netherlands, French General Bernard Janvier—secretly met at Javornik in Croatia.

About 15,000 men and women gathered in Srebrenica, the UN-recognized safe area in Drina Valley, on 12 July, to protest against the war. The women were taken to army camps and thrown to thousands of soldiers to be raped. About 8,500 men and teenagers were hacked to death with all kinds of weapons in seven days. Not a single teenager or man gathered there could survive 13 July 1995, which was forever marked in history as the Srebrenica massacre. Their bodies were taken a few kilometres away in army trucks and municipal garbage carriages and buried in mass graves. Serbian commander Ratko Mladić became infamous as the 'Butcher of Bosnia'. UN Secretary-General Kofi Annan later recognized the incident as genocide. Later, the International Court of Justice, too, echoed the same opinion, citing it as the largest barbaric incident in Europe since World War II.

International powers took the Srebrenica massacre seriously. The army of a country could not continue waging war against its own countrymen. The Bosnia-Herzegovina agreement had been drafted since 1992. A peace agreement was proposed on 1 November 1995 at the Wright-Patterson Air Force Base.

In Paris, on 14 December 1995, Serbian President Milošević signed the Dayton Agreement. It was also signed by Croatian President Franjo Tudjman and Bosnian President Alija Izetbegović. To ensure peace, NATO posted 60,000 troops in charge of peacekeeping operations across the country. This agreement ended a 43-month war, immortalized in history as the Balkan Conflict. But the horrors of this civil war will remain etched in the global consciousness for generations to come. The country is still struggling to get back on its feet in the aftermath of this carnage.

At the United Nations Security Council meeting on 21 December 1995, it was decided (1035/95) that Bosnia would be handed over to the IPTF for peacekeeping, in a programme called the United Nations Mission in Bosnia and Herzegovina (UNMIBH). Officers were requisitioned from all the member countries. Answering the UN's call, 46 countries sent their officers to UNMIBH. This International Community Police was tasked with the reconstruction and restructuring of Bosnia.

In addition to European countries, others like USA, India, Pakistan, Bangladesh, China, Fiji, Malaysia, Egypt, Jordan,

Nigeria and Ghana joined the mission. The IPTF had very specific duties. Along with maintaining law and order, it was responsible for restructuring the police system, increasing the people's engagement with the local police, arranging training for them, enacting legislation, raising awareness about human rights violations, providing legal counsel to local governments and ensuring fair voting.

Four

The week-long induction training included various classes. For a lover of the past, what fascinated me the most was the history of Bosnia. Geographical details, socio-economic status, human behaviour, literary culture, their sufferings during the war, etc., were all a part of our curriculum.

In the middle of our training, we were informed of a driving test. Four monitors were engaged from different countries to conduct this test. Turkey's monitor Omar Jeniff came to take our group test. He looked me over and asked, 'Which part of India are you from?'

'East…Calcutta. Do you know about India?' I asked.

'I know very little. My great great grandmother was an Indian. I have only been to Bombay, with my father, when I was little. I remember throngs of people and lots of cars in the city. I don't remember much else.' He took us to a secluded street across Downtown Road in Sarajevo, where he tested us on our driving skills.

Eventually, he said, 'You and your friend, Siddhartha have passed. But some of your friends could not succeed. Only nine out of fifteen passed the test, the rest will not get a driving licence.'

'Is it so? Then how will they travel in this country?'

'Sorry, there is no way! They have to depend on others. I am sure they haven't come here to kill people in road accidents.'

Realizing that we couldn't appeal to him without coming off as rule breakers ourselves, we simply stared at him.

Understanding our state of mind, he said, 'The test will

be held again within a month. Only after passing the driving test will they get their licence. However, if they fail again, they will face repatriation. So, if necessary, they can train at the local driving school.'

I returned to the MHQ to collect my driving licence.

'You have to show your licence to take a car from the unit. The car will not start unless you swipe this licence in the control panel of the dashboard. Therefore, a car taken under the name of another person will not work unless you have your own licence.' Omar said.

On the last day of training, the IPTF Commissioner, an American officer, came to us for introductions. 'What more can be learned about a war-torn country with such a bloodied history of conflict in a week of lectures? Dive into your work with a neutral mind. You will learn more about this place as you work here.' In a softer, almost conspiratorial voice, he added, 'I would rather ask you to share your experiences with my office.' Shaking hands with everyone, he invited us to a tea party. There, I learnt that I had been posted at an IPTF station called Modriča, near the Croatian border in the north. It was almost 200 kilometres from Sarajevo.

Dividing Bosnia into six parts, a total of 48 IPTF stations, under the six regional headquarters, were established to meet the requirements of the Dayton Agreement. The cities of Bihać, Tuzla, Sarajevo and Mostar were Muslim-dominated, whereas Banja Luka and Doboj were Serb-dominated. Bosnia-Herzegovina was being governed by two completely different entities. About 52 per cent was being controlled by the Federation of Bosnia and Herzegovina, and the remaining 48 per cent by the Republika Srpska. While the federation was headed by Muslims and accompanied by Croats, the Republika Srpska entirely comprised Serbians. However, the population was mixed. Bordering Croatia and Serbia was another district, Brčko, which boasted a separate administrative system and identity entirely.

I was told that the beautiful river Sava encircled the entire city of Brčko. There were numerous restaurants and nightclubs on the Sava, mostly accommodated in big launches. The weekends were rather colourful there. But no Asians were posted there. Only Europeans and Americans enjoyed its beauty.

'Why don't they post Asians there?' I looked at the others inquisitively.

Mesut, a Jordanian official, said, 'There are three IPTF stations in Brčko, with a total of around hundred international officers, but not a single one of them is Asian. What do you think that means? They must believe that Americans and Europeans have the sole right to such pleasures.'

'Couldn't it simply be a coincidence?'

Anger flared up in Mesut's eyes, 'If you have the guts for it, the IPTF commissioner is still in his chamber. Why don't you ask him? Come, I'll accompany you.'

Before I could grasp the implications, the flash of anger was gone from his eyes. Noticing my hesitation, Mesut asked, 'Would you spend money in a nightclub like the American-Europeans do?' Reading my silence, he continued, 'You wouldn't waste your hard-earned money, would you? You would rather save every penny—think about your family, the future of your children. Instead, if you want to waste your money on wine, women and cheap revelries, if you have come here on a mission to sleep with Slavic beauties, then, by all means, I would like to know why they will not post you at Brčko!'

I was flustered by such a sarcastic argument. I refused to believe that mission policy could be this discriminatory or that people associating themselves with the UN could take up a foreign assignment with such intentions. Hiding my surprise, I replied, 'Look, Mesut, we decide our own ethics. We set our own boundaries. Law and ethics are two different issues. The law is the same for everyone, but ethics is a personal choice.'

Mesut smiled, though not entirely mollified, and said, 'Whatever you say, but there is not a single Asian in those three IPTF stations. It cannot be a coincidence.'

I grinned, 'Today is my eighth day in this country. It is not the right time to protest. Give me some time, I will protest if I find anything wrong. I am a Bengali. Rebellion runs in my blood.'

We had arrived in Bosnia the day after Christmas. Sarajevo had embraced its shivering winter and warmed up to the year-end festivities. The bus that had carried us from the airport on our first day, took us back and forth between Owaza Hotel and the MHQ, as per schedule. On these journeys, I would see the bar-restaurants decorated with glitters, tinsels, stars and a paraphernalia of festive items. While some of the trainees often visited the restaurants and bars near our hotel, overcome by the cold, I preferred to spend my evenings in the hotel lobby, snow-covered lawn garden or my cosy room. However, at everyone's request, after dinner, on New Year's Eve, I reached the ballroom of Hotel Owaza.

Preparations had been going on since the evening. The hotel owner as well as all the staff were celebrating indiscriminately. As I stood by, watching everyone dance with reckless abandon, a housekeeping girl approached me. She hugged my waist and pushed herself to my chest. But disheartened by my lack of response, she soon left me to join the crowd.

Five

On the ninth day, everyone packed their suitcases and got ready to be dispatched to their respective places of posting. At two o'clock, a car arrived from Modriča to receive me. The Nepali officer, Labahari Shreshtha, alighted from the car and shook my hands with genuine pleasure. Labahari looked like an Assamese wrestler, with a sombre face.

Siddhartha had left for Zenica a while back. Before leaving, I told him that I wished we could have stayed together for the rest of our tenure.

Siddhartha assured me that he would try to get me posted in Zenica, where the Muslim population was higher. Modriča, on the other hand, was Serb dominated. He tried to lure me with all the history that Zenica promised.

Carrying my large suitcase and luggage, I got into the front seat of the Toyota. All the cars here were left drive.

'Put on your seatbelt. It's a heinous crime in this country,' Labahari said in English.

I rushed to fasten my seatbelt and blurted out, 'Not wearing a seatbelt is a heinous crime in all countries.'

Starting the car, Labahari spoke in fluent Hindi, 'Do you need something like groceries or fruit juice or chicken pili or salami? Modriča is a village. Things are not good. The things that are available are more expensive than in this place.'

I shook my head and said, 'I went shopping yesterday, I have everything I need.'

'Will you cook or eat at the hotel?' Labahari probed. But before I could answer, he continued, 'During the day, of course, you will not have time to cook due to work pressure. But at night, you'll have plenty of time to cook in peace.'

'I will do as much as time permits. I didn't plan anything specific,' I replied.

'I have some shopping to complete. There is a market complex ahead. I will stop there. You may come along if you have any second thoughts about shopping.'

I spotted the Cosmo Complex on the right side of the road as we proceeded further. After entering the premises and parking the car at the specified place, we got out.

Labahari said, 'It's warm inside. There are beautiful girls there too. So, even if you don't have any shopping to do, I don't think going to the market will go in vain. Anyway, it's freezing outside.'

The complex was packed with a wide range of groceries, including items like various kinds of fishes, meats, fruits and juices. But most dazzling were the beauties across the complex. Some were sales girls and some customers. Thus far, my idea about Bosnian people was formed entirely by observing the support staff at the MHQ. But I was yet to meet the common people in crowds. The first time I realized what Balkan beauty is was in that complex. I was left mesmerized by their lithe bodies, supple skin, sharp eyes and cascading hair. The men here were also beautiful, but gigantic. Men over six feet were quite common here, and my pride at being 5'11" was shattered soon after I arrived in Bosnia.

Labahari returned with his trolley and joined the queue at the payment counter. I walked towards him. Seeing me from a distance, he said, 'I am done. But we have to wait in queue.' Nodding my head, I stood at some distance. A young woman, about 5'8" tall, approached me from a corner and asked in clear English, 'May I help you?'

I looked at her, surprised. Maybe Tagore had her in mind

when he described a woman as a *mayabono biharini horini* (deer of the enchanted forest). She came and quietly stood close to me. I could smell her perfume. I looked around to make sure she was indeed talking to me. I glanced at Labahari and saw him shake his head fiercely. I might have mimicked his gesture, as the girl smiled up at me.

Extending her hand, she said, 'Hi, I'm Zinnia, do you want to feel me from the inside?'

'Sorry, I can't understand you,' I shook my head.

'You don't need to understand me. It's simple, I have a place nearby, let's move there.'

I was rendered speechless.

'Just feel me, play with me and pay me $20 for an hour,' Zinnia added without hesitation.

'You are very beautiful, but I am not in the mood to play with you right now. I'm sorry,' I replied.

She extended her hand towards me. So, I reached out as well. Zinnia took my hand in her soft warm ones and squeezed it fleetingly., 'Okay, next time,' she whispered and left.

Labahari appeared by my side with his fresh purchases.

'The girl is very beautiful, what do you say?' Labahari almost startled me, 'But we would have been late had you gone with her. At least two hours, I assume!'

'What do you mean, eh?' I looked at him with accusing eyes.

'I mean, if you had agreed to avail of her hospitality, she might have taken you to a nearby hotel or nightclub, then to bed, you know. It would have taken at least two hours,' said Labahari in a light tone that didn't seem to match his serious face. By then, it was too late. We had already walked up to the parking lot.

'Ishh, what a shame!' I was repulsed by his words.

'Are you really ashamed?' Labahari gave me a sidelong glance and continued, 'But after spending a few days here, you won't be.' As he got into the car, he charged at me, 'Surely, you were standing there looking at girls like a novice? Why else would she target you? The girls followed your gaze. It is evident that you are not from this country. There is always a demand when you come from outside.'

'You are not a native here either. It is evident from your appearance. So, what is your demand to these ladies?' I settled into the passenger seat.

'I don't have the charisma to attract such girls. Anyway, I do not have the confidence to handle them either. But they will swarm around you like bees.'

'Hey, I have noticed that the number of women here is more than that of men, unlike in our country. But surely, it cannot be as you say,' I protested.

With a chuckle, he changed the gear and increased the speed. After a companionable silence, he said, 'The fact is that the civil war of the last decade has completely destroyed the economy. For $25, even girls like fairies agree to spend a few hours with strangers. Look at them. Taste them to your heart's content, my friend. You could bang your head against a wall and still not find such beauties back in Calcutta!'

He might have said it with levity, but the grim truth in his voice weighed on my chest. I trained my eyes outside the window.

The snowfall started about 25 kilometres into the journey. Worried, I asked, 'Hope you have sufficient practise of driving on icy roads?'

'Not exactly. You see, my house is in a village some 10 kilometres from Kathmandu, Nepal. We never experience snowfall. I joined this mission a month ago. It wasn't snowing when I arrived, neither was there much need to drive. But for the last three days, there has been considerable snowfall. This is my third day driving on ice. Today is the first time that I am driving such a long distance on icy roads.'

I stared at him in utter shock. 'How will we cover 200 kilometres of such icy road?'

Labahari reassured me. 'Don't worry, the wheels are chained, they won't skid. The car is going at a snail's pace of 40 kmph; I can handle it even if it skids.'

As the car crawled up the road, eddies of snow seemed to impede our visibility. Snow had piled up by the side of the road. I slouched into my seat, awash with fear. Noticing my condition, Labahari said, 'There is a can of beer in the back seat. Have some. It will make you feel better.'

I shook my head and said, 'I don't consume alcohol.'

He took his eyes off the road and stared at me. 'Are you from proper Calcutta or from a remote village?'

'My home is in a village in Medinipur district, about 125 kilometres from Calcutta. Why this question all of a sudden?' I asked Labahari.

'One of my cousins visits Calcutta from time to time to supply glass and electronic goods to Fancy Market there. From what I have heard, I guessed that if you were born and raised in Calcutta, you wouldn't consider beer alcohol.'

When we reached the IPTF station in Modriča, it was about eight in the evening. The station was deserted, except a young woman with bright golden hair. Seeing us, she came forward and hugged me. Touching both my cheeks with her warm ones, she said, '*Dobre dosli* (welcome)! I'm Suzanne Grabovic, your LA (language assistant). I will take you to your rented apartment,' she said in English.

Suzanne looked extremely familiar, but I couldn't place her in my memory. This was my first visit to Bosnia, and it was unlikely that she had ever been to Calcutta. It amused me when I finally figured it out. I had seen her in Hindi movies. Had her hair been black instead of blonde, she would have looked identical to the Indian actress Saira Banu.

As she hugged me and touched me on the cheek, I became a bit shy, and seeing me hunched over in embarrassment, Labahari said, '*Sharmaiye maat. Yahan yeh sab chalta hai. Station kabka khali ho gaya hai. Apko apka flat dikhayegi yeh ladki, is liye ruki hui hai* (Don't be shy. This gesture is normal here. She has been waiting for you in this empty station to take you to your new apartment).'

Labahari accompanied me to the rented apartment nearby. The owner of the house, Drakomir Petrovic, and his beautiful daughter, Srietlana, came out and greeted me. Half of the first floor had been rented out by the Modriča station for my accommodation. It was a clean, well-decorated flat with central heating. The rent seemed cheap at 350 DM per month. Drakomir and Srietlana helped me carry my luggage to the first floor.

Suzanne came to see me once I was settled in the apartment. She lived in a village called Prada, approximately 30 kilometres from there.

'How will you go home?' I asked her.

'I have my car parked at the station,' she said, and without another word, she walked out into the dark.

Six

I was quite hungry as I climbed up to the first-floor apartment. I had noticed a shop next door. I rushed down again, and in my hurry, I lost my footing and fell down on the slippery ice. As I was cushioned with layers of clothes, I sustained no injury. Clambering to my feet and wiping the ice off my jacket, I felt someone's eyes on me. I looked up towards the window of the house and found Srietlana staring at me with a mischievous smile. I waved at her, embarrassed.

The old Serbian shopkeeper was about to close up by the time I reached the shop. I quickly bought some vegetables and returned to my apartment. I had planned to take my meals at the hotel for the first few days and start cooking only once I settled into a routine. But seeing the vast array of items at the Cosmo Complex, as well as Labahari's suggestions made me change my mind. I fished out the rice, moong dal and pressure cooker that I had brought from Calcutta.

I was debating whether to take it off the oven after two whistles when I was startled by the persistent ringing of the bell. I opened the door and saw Drakomir, the owner of the house. He barged in, seemingly agitated, saying something in Bosnian that I could not understand. When the third whistle blew, he rushed out of the room and peered in through the door, assessing the pressure cooker warily. I finally understood the issue. Moving away, I switched off the oven. Drakomir had never seen a pressure cooker before. I tried to explain, through gestures, that it was a cooking utensil. I would later learn that pressure cookers were not used in Bosnia at all.

He gave me a toothy grin, the tension leaving his body. He patted my back and shook his head, muttering, '*Dobre dobre* (good good).' I invited him to join me for dinner. Through a polite gesture he turned me down and promised to catch up another time. I whipped up an omelette and sat down with the khichdi that I had prepared. It tasted like elixir. I wanted to pat myself on the back for creating such a masterpiece. After dinner, I cleaned up and turned in for the night.

In the morning, Labahari offered me a ride, although the station was about 300 metres away. I reached to find it crowded. The station commander approached me. He shook my hand fervently, with a big smile. 'I am Vettori from Rassya,' he said. I noticed how in the mouth of a Russian, Russia becomes the dental fricative 'Rassya'. I introduced myself with a smile. About 30 police officers from different countries and a dozen local LAs shook hands with me as well. The LAs were interpreters who aided in communication when interacting with the local people. They also translated into English any complaint lodged in the local language, which was usually the case.

Once the introductions ended, the commander sat down for the briefing session, which primarily involved allocating tasks to the different teams and getting a general verbal update on the previous day's work. I learned that this Modriča IPTF station had eight different teams, each monitoring a different police station. A team consisted of three officers from different countries, with one LA and one vehicle each. There were three members of the specialized STOP (Special Trafficking Operations Programme) team as well. There was another specialized team dealing with human rights, but it had no members at the moment. I was made its first member.

'At the moment, there is nobody else in Human Rights. So, you will have to work alone on this assignment. Your job is to enquire into the complaints of common people and submit reports and assignment on some special tasks from the MHQ. I am mailing your name to the Human Rights branch at MHQ.' Pausing to think, he said, 'There is a mass grave in Vukosavlje. Today is its excavation. Yo should move there.

I agreed to oversee the UN's mass grave excavation at Vukosavlje on behalf of the international community.

The commander handed me a car key and said, 'Take this car. The LA from yesterday, Suzanne, will accompany you.' I suspected that Vettori had already planned to put me in Human Rights, even before my posting.

Suzanne informed me that Vukosavlje was almost 30 kilometres from our station.

'Do you know the location of the mass grave?' I asked her.

'I don't. But first we'll go to the Vukosavlje local police station. They will find an escort to take us to the spot. Wait. Let me call them before we leave.'

Suzanne slipped into the passenger seat as I turned the key in the ignition. I said, 'I have never driven on such slippery roads before. Will you help me drive?'

'Yes, I'll guide you,' she said confidently as I eased out of the parking. 'Go slow and don't use the brake. Change the gear to regulate your speed and ease into a stop during emergencies.'

Noticing the bewilderment on my face, she explained, 'I have my own car and I've been driving for five years. But we're not allowed to drive a UN vehicle.'

After a while, I turned down from the main road, into a smaller road. It curved along the banks of the river Bosna. The serpentine road followed the whims of the river as she dipped down in places and swelled up at others, foaming and frothing through rapid currents, carrying snow and ice along the way. The naked trees by the road drooped their bleached branches under the weight of snow. The sun shown in a brilliant blue sky, stitched through with patches of white clouds. It was a perfect day. I could smell the sweet perfume of the beautiful girl seated beside me. Suzanne chatted away in all her youthful exuberance. It was the perfect setting for romance. But I was driving with my jaw clenched and knuckles white on the steering wheel. A thin layer of perspiration had formed on my forehead as I guided the car up a hillock.

Suzanne was narrating how she was Serbian but didn't hate Muslims. 'All humans are equal,' she explained with a smile. Midway through a master's degree in English literature, she received a call from the UN and has been working as an LA ever since. She received a handsome remuneration and wanted to complete her master's as soon as the UN mission concluded. She was 27 and hoped to settle in the US by her mid-thirties. Although I was listening to her, my eyes were trained straight on the road.

Without warning, Suzanne shouted, 'Look to the left!'

Frightened, I instinctively hit the brakes. The car skidded about 7 or 8 feet on the ice and swerved back down the road. I pulled the handbrakes and jumped out of the car. Suzanne had also slipped out of the car. She checked the wheels and said, 'I'm sorry, I didn't think you would panic. I probably shouted a little louder than I should have. Try to ease the car up. I think it can still be manoeuvered back on the road.'

I was shaken. 'What if the car falls into the river? It is a long drop and the riverbank is dangerously steep.' I was shaking, in fear or shock, I did not know.

'No, no, it will not fall into the river. Let me help you.' Suzanne was quite agile. She found some rocks and placed them behind the wheels to keep them from rolling down. She guided me back into the driver's seat and said, 'Now gently put pressure on the accelerator. Feather light. Otherwise, the wheels might have a false run.'

Frightened, I started the car. After a few attempts, it inched up on the road.

Suzanne jumped about and clapped her hands like a little girl. 'Well done, well done!' She ran up and jumped into her seat again. As she got into the car, I let out a huge sigh and asked, 'What were you showing me to the left?'

Closing the door, she pointed out through my window, 'That is TešanjKa. Look there, can you see that village above it?'

I saw a snow-covered mound that looked like a house or two. 'In 1994, the Serbian army raided that village and set it on fire. There were about 300 houses. Twelve hundred Muslims lived there. That's Novi Grad. Nobody knows where they went…' Suzanne's voice broke as she said this.

'You mean, they disappeared? Where did they go?' I asked her, bewildered.

She nodded slowly, 'Um… I don't know. Nobody knows …'

I felt a growing pit in my stomach. 'Where could they have gone? Surely many survived? No one returned here, even after so many years?'

'Not everyone is dead, some are still alive. Maybe they're scattered now. I hope they come back one day.'

'But it has been six years since the war ended. They should have returned by now. The IPTF is here now.' I quipped.

'It is easy to say these things. But we can't fathom the trauma of those who saw their children, brothers or husbands being shot, hacked or burnt alive in front of their eyes. Can you imagine the pain of those who witnessed their wives, daughters and sisters raped?' Suzanne's cheeks were moist with tears as she spoke.

I turned to look at her as she pulled out a handkerchief from her bag and gently wiped her eyes with it.

We drove up a lonely snow-covered hill. As we turned east at the corner, its reflection dazzled me. It felt like we were alone in this vast expansive silence. I gave Suzanne time to compose herself as I drove quietly down the road.

'I had two friends who lived there—Ajmira and Munira. We went to college together for almost two years. That day, they disappeared.' After a while, she spoke again in a fragile voice, 'Who knows, maybe someday they will return and embrace me from behind, like they used to.'

Reluctant to break the delicate moment, I said, 'They will definitely return. Gradually, Novi Grad will become its old dynamic self. It will take time. But on snowy evenings, grandparents will tell stories to their grandchildren again.'

Suzanne had calmed down by now.

'Will you take me to Novi Grad one day?' I asked her.

'I can take you there on our way back today, if you are ready to walk for half an hour,' she replied with a smile.

I immediately agreed. It would be a rare opportunity to see the results of the destruction that I had come here to repair.

A few minutes later, we arrived at the Vukosavlje police station. The station commander saw our car approach and came out to greet us. Despite the grin on his face, he looked like a WWF wrestler. He clasped my hands and said, '*Dobar Dan* (hello).' He took us inside his chamber. The introductions were made by Suzanne. That there were forty-odd people in the station, yet no one knew English, did not escape me. The station commander ushered us to a corner of the chamber that smelt of coffee. He returned shortly with two coffee mugs for Suzanne and me.

'Will you not drink with us?' I asked.

'I had mine while waiting for you.'

The car had slipped off the road. It took us some time to bring it back on the road. Thereafter, I drove slowly for fear of further mishaps on the snow.

Suzanne winked at me. I gathered that she had said

something about the Modriča IPTF station instead of translating my response.

One sip of the coffee and I almost gagged. I had never tasted something that bitter and foul before. From time to time, I did pretend to drink from the mug, but I refused to take another sip. Suzanne, on the other hand, finished her coffee with great satisfaction. I asked Suzanne whether the officers here spoke English. She seemed unsurprised by the fact that they did not. It was a trivial matter to her. She explained that 95 per cent Bosnians didn't know English. All their education, and consequently books, were in their native language.

On learning of my nationality, the commander said that he had heard of Gandhi, Nehru, and Kabir Bedi, who had acted in the movie *Sandokan*.

Our conversation, mediated by Suzanne, was cut short by the arrival of an investigating judge, two forensic experts and representatives from the Ministry of Interior (like our Ministry of Home Affairs). We left soon after. The road was flat and clean, with snow piled up on both sides. The snow and icicles hung from the trees like white bats. The landscape was entirely white. We drove for fifteen minutes and arrived at a large, frozen fountain. German SFOR (Stabilizing Force) troops had already cordoned off the area.

Seven

As soon as we arrived, the dozers started digging. After about 3 feet, they unearthed a piece of blanket. Suspecting that there might be a skeleton after that, two people clambered down and continued digging with a spade and a shovel. Slowly, removing the soil with care, they uncovered parts of leather jackets, and then some hair and synthetic garments. Underneath them all were the bones. In my naivety, I assumed that the skeletons would be arranged one after the other individually. But it was soon evident that several bodies were piled up within a small area. I could not fathom how corpses could be handled with such callousness. I found myself trembling, in the cold or with horror, I could not tell.

Two people carried out the bones, one by one, and dumped them on a tarpaulin next to the grave site. The forensic experts reconstructed the skeletons in a couple of hours. Sixteen such skeletons were arranged in a row. From the size of three of them, it was easy to deduce that they belonged to children. Forensic experts concluded that nine of them were female.

The police asked, 'How do you know the gender of these skeletons?'

Suzanne immediately took to translating the conversation for me.

One of the forensic experts pointed at the pelvic bones of the skeletons and explained that structurally the pelvic girdle of the nine skeletons were wider than the rest. The skeletons were also shorter in length. This observation was in keeping with the physiology of females.

I noticed several dissatisfied faces. They were not convinced by this explanation. The station commander took some pictures of the grave site and the skeletons. When no one was looking, I picked up a few pieces of clothing and a little dark soil and put them in an envelope, swiftly returning it to my jacket pocket.

My heart grew heavy with sorrow, even as my mind grappled with unanswered questions. It was easy to deduce that these people were gathered from a village nearby. Who were they? Why were they killed? What savagery could bring human beings to murder innocent children in cold blood? How did they die? What instruments were used to kill them? Were they tortured before being killed? Did they put up a fight?

Some of my questions would be answered only after the post-mortem but some would forever remain unanswered. And finally, the most personal question, what would I have done in such a situation? Some of their family members must be alive, so a few of my questions had the possibility of finding answers. But some of the answers I sought were lost to history. I turned away from the skeletons as my eyes grew moist.

I bid farewell to the people of the Vukosavlje police station who were packing the skeletons into large separate bags. Once we were inside the car, I turned to Suzanne and said, 'Let's go to Novi Grad.'

On the way back, Suzanne told me to park the car at the Vukosavlje market. She slipped out and returned with two paper bags and Coca-Cola cans. With the first bite of my sandwich, I realized how hungry I was.

While crossing a bridge, Suzanne pointed out, 'We're crossing the Bosna.'

I peeked over the side of the railing, and the languid river shimmered at me. I asked Suzanne, 'At the police station, why didn't you translate what I said about skidding off the road? You were making some gestures. I did not quite follow what you were trying to convey to me.'

'You shouldn't have said it in that manner,' said Suzanne. 'So, I cooked up an excuse about extra work at Modriča station as the reason for our delay.'

'Um, got it.' I shook my head.

She sighed and continued, as if explaining to a child. 'You are representing the international community on behalf of the UN. You shouldn't confess to your lack of driving skills. Why would you tell them that? People here would laugh at you. I won't tolerate that.'

'Hmm,' I sighed as I glanced at Suzanne's face. A light smile played on her lips that dazzled me with its brilliance, brighter than the sun outside.

The sun had dipped close to the western horizon by the time we reached Novi Grad. 'We have to get off here. Rest of the way is on foot. It will take less than half an hour,' said Suzanne. So, I parked the car and stepped out. The blanket of snow over the landscape was set aglow by the rays of the setting sun. The tranquillity and gentle breeze soothed my restless thoughts.

'A small culvert in front of the village is broken,' Suzanne said. 'The villagers blew up the culvert so that the Serbian army vehicles could not reach the village. Yet, hundreds of Serbian soldiers raided the village on foot.'

I followed Suzanne to the village. Tall trees like emaciated sentinels stood guarding Novi Grad, decked in their winter whites. They seemed happy to have visitors after so long. I knew that riddled with bullet holes, rendered invisible from years of winters, these trees still held the painful memories of all the atrocities they had been forced to witness. The entire village, almost in ruins, was buried under layers of snow and ice. Only a handful of houses were still left standing there. Suzanne pointed to the one on the right and said, 'That one belonged to Munira's family.'

The house she pointed at was dilapidated yet somehow left standing. The door to the main entrance had been destroyed, though the inner rooms seemed intact. Invited in by the whispering wind, I moved towards the house. Suzanne grabbed my hand and held me back. 'My God, what are you doing?' Surprised, I looked at her. There was fear written on her face.

Suzanne asked, 'Have you been taught nothing during your training? Don't you know there could be a live landmine there?'

Annoyed, I said, 'Yes, but the land mines or booby traps are always planted in the important places. This haunted house can't be that important!'

'No, sir, there are thousands of mines planted on Bosnian soil, in orchards, shrines and other unexpected locations. The lesser-known fact is that while the armies planted mines to stop the opposition, the common people planted improvised, smuggled mines in their homes, as self-defence. SFOR has deactivated and removed mines from the more important places, but such places are still more than likely to have them.'

'Sorry, I didn't know that.'

'It's okay, be careful next time,' said Suzanne.

I walked up a mound with Suzanne and asked, 'Can you find me some flowers?'

'Flowers? Where will you find flowers in this snow-covered ruin? What do you want with them?'

'I want to pay my respect to the dead here.'

'You will not find flowers here.' She was hesitant. She held out her beautiful silk scarf and said, 'This has lots of flowers in it.' On seeing me hesitate, she urged me, 'Please take it, I won't mind. If you are feeling bad about taking it, you can always buy me one from Sarajevo.'

We had reached the centre of the village. I sat down by the road and started piling snow into an altar. Kneeling down, I took the scarf from Suzanne and spread it out on the top with great care. I took off my gloves and pressed my palms over it. Suzanne picked up more snow with both hands and whispered while depositing it on the altar, 'The scarf, too, will blow away with the wind, like this village was by machine gun'.

When I got up after paying my respects to the dead of Novi Grad, my cheeks were wet. I walked brusquely towards the car with my face turned down. In the deafening silence of my surroundings, the hills, too, wore a funereal white.

'We have to return by another road. It is a little detour. But it's not as steep and has less snow,' Suzanne whispered.

I got in the car and started the vehicle. We took the detour to the Modriča-Sarajevo Highway on our way back. Suzanne said that she was hungry. As soon as we reached Pelajica, a small marketplace, she instructed me to stop the car. Suzanne soon returned with two packets and two cans of Coca-Cola. Boarding the car, she said, 'Try this.' I peered into the packet to find what looked like our Moghlai paratha.

'What is it?'

'That's *burek*. It is popular with the Indians and Pakistanis,' she explained. 'It is available with both beef and chicken fillings. But, I guess, Indians eat more chicken, so I brought chicken burek for you.' I bit into it. As I had suspected, the minced meat in the paratha did not have any spices. The only flavour was from copious amounts of garlic and tomato ketchup. Despite that, it was rather tasty. Eyeing the can of Coca-Cola, I asked, 'How much of this stuff do you drink all day?'

'Coca-Cola and Pepsi have replaced water, especially in winter. With many snacks and street food, Coke is free.' I was fishing for money in my pocket when Suzanne shook her head. 'Why don't you buy me lunch tomorrow instead?'

As I sat there sipping Coca-Cola, Suzanne said, 'This is a different way to Modriča, the light is dimming, and there's snow on the road. You must be cautious. But I tend to blabber on when in a car. So, I can sit in the back seat if you prefer. Wouldn't want to distract you.'

'Not necessary.' I shook my head and explained, 'This morning was my first time driving on snow. I miscalculated. But I think I've gotten a hang of this now.' I eased the car back on the road. Suzanne was dozing off beside me. The mass grave of Vukosavlje haunted my thoughts again. Rotten meat, decomposed clothes and black soil felt heavy in my pocket. Sixteen corpses in a grave! I come from the land of the Ramayana and the Mahabharata, the great epics celebrating the pinnacles of human civilization. But the evidence of brutality that I witnessed in that grave site today left me questioning the inviolable goodness of humanity. Could the great Roman Empire, which had left its footprints all over Eastern Europe, have envisaged a future of such senseless bloodshed? I sighed, the weight in my chest returning. I dropped the half-empty Coca-Cola can out through the window as I drove back to Modriča.

Suzanne spoke quietly, with her eyes still closed. 'You have suffered greatly today, haven't you? Two incidents in a row on your first day at work.' Egged on by my silence, she continued, 'I, too, had a hard time at first. I have become mechanical now. I have also experienced much of the horrors through personal tragedies. One day, I will tell you everything. Even my own father was not spared from this war.'

I looked at her curiously and asked, 'But aren't you Serbian?'

'Yes, but during the ethnic cleansing, the Bosnians retaliated against the Serbs as best as they could. They resorted to covert attacks to avenge the deaths of their loved ones. In this manner, they targeted as many people from the Serbian army as they could. My father was a deputy commander of a troop in the Serbian army, but he chose voluntary retirement over the senseless conflict. In spite of that, he was victimized by angry Bosnians. I'll take you to our house; you'll see how ordinary we are. We have no enmity with anybody.'

Comforted by my silence, Suzanne continued, 'When the rumour of war spread through the country, my father was dead against it. That is why he took voluntary retirement from the army. He knew a war was imminent, but he wanted no part of it. He took to cultivating vegetables and fishing in the Bosna. In 1994, I was fresh out of school. One summer morning, he dropped me off at my college and went fishing. He said he would pick me up at the end of the day.

'I still remember, the teacher was explaining "Cowards die many times before their deaths. The valiant never taste of death but once" from *Julius Caesar*, by Shakespeare, when a neighbour came to inform me that my father was found seriously wounded in the water of Bosna. I rushed to the hospital with him. I found my father lying on a hospital bed, his face a mask of calmness. There was no trace of pain on his face. There was no life in his body either. Twenty-two injuries riddled his entire body, with at least ten on both hands. Hands that had dropped the rifle and taken up farming. It all ended in a couple of years,' Suzanne's voice choked with grief.

Looking away, I asked in a calm voice, 'Will you take me to your home one day? I want to know more.'

With a little restraint Suzanne's mood changed immediately. She asked, 'You really want to see my home?'

'Yes, of course,' I quipped.

'I'll take you there soon.'

When I parked the car near the IPTF station, it was dark outside. Suzanne bid me goodbye and left the parking lot.

The station was almost deserted. A Nigerian monitor, Charles, sat at the computer, sending emails. I asked him, 'Do you know where the station commander is?'

He looked up at me with an unreadable expression on his face but didn't reply. I repeated myself. This time, his eyes focussed on me and he seemed to take me in. He spoke in a hoarse voice, 'From which country are you?'

On mentioning India, his expression changed a little, as he asked, 'You want me to find the station commander for you?'

I shook my head. 'I only want to know whether you have seen him around.'

Charles burst out guffawing, 'Hey man, how would I know? I don't drink with him. You'll probably find him in the bar, drinking with his Russian friends. But if you want to drink at his expenses, then you're out of luck. That honour is reserved for the Ukrainian girls.'

'Hey, no, I was looking for him, since he told me to report to him.'

His bushy brows shot up. He said, 'You have come this evening to report about work? What are you trying to do, single-handedly save this forsaken country? Don't you know the commander doesn't come to the station after morning?'

'Sorry, I joined this station today.'

'Yes, you look new.' Charles got up from his chair, hugged me and said, 'I'm going home now, I can't offer you a drink, but you can join me if you want to taste some delicious beef soup.'

'No, sorry. I was out since morning. It has been a long day. I'm tired. I'll go to your place another day. I want to sleep now.'

'See you tomorrow.'

I was in a bitter mood, and talking to Charles made it worse. I left the car at the station premises and walked to my rented flat. My first day at the UN mission had officially ended.

Eight

Srietlana opened the door when I rang the bell.

'Good evening,' I smiled. I dared to imagine a world where Karishma Tanna would open the door for me. But her face was much brighter than our native Karishma.

Srietlana covered her mouth with her fingers spread over her face and said with a smile, '*Nema English. Tee locala uchiti, teme prizateliu.*' The sorrow of not being able to communicate with such a beauty for my simple lack of knowledge of her language will haunt me for a while. I later asked Suzanne to translate the sentence for me, without disclosing the identity of the speaker. Srietlana had said, 'I don't know English. If you learn the local language, then I can be your friend.'

I thought I would take a bath after returning home. But I changed my mind the moment I stepped into the bathroom. The split heater in the washroom was not working. There was ice on the window. So, I switched on the geyser and returned to the bedroom. The central heating there was working fine.

I quickly changed into a fresh pair of clothes and washed up the best I could. Then, I took the soil-filled envelope out of the pocket of my jacket. The next moment, I felt the dead crowding into my room. The dead of Vukosavlje and Novi Grad. They seemed grateful for being acknowledged and released from their cramped graves, for being recognized and honoured. My heart felt heavy again. But that heaviness now found release through tears that stained my face, flowing freely in the privacy of my room. I had planned to cook hotchpotch for dinner but discarded the idea. I was too numb to move. I munched on some biscuits from my suitcase, but they tasted bitter. I retreated under my covers, with thoughts of Novi Grad haunting my mind.

If I closed my eyes, I could see the downpour on the night the Serbian army attacked the village. The rain had softened the soil. Now the moon hung high in the sky, as a cold breeze blew through the village, whispering of death. There were a few hours left till dawn. Army vans were moving slowly along the rough asphalt road, a hunting owl guided them towards the houses. The village was asleep. All was quiet, except the crunching of the wheels. Army soldiers with identical expressionless, square-jawed faces and hollow eyes looked on from inside the vans, machine guns in hand and assault rifles on their shoulders. The vans came to a halt and the soldiers jumped out, cursing under their breaths. Three army engineers moved ahead with mine sweepers, while the soldiers lined up after them, marching up Tešanjka, shattering the quiet of the night. I could imagine the echoes of their footsteps. They were determined.

I saw them attack the village, a deluge of chaos and destruction. The collective screams of the villagers trying to escape their fate. The echoing staccato of machine guns, the thud of bodies collapsing to the ground, the smell of blood and gunpowder mixing with the fragrance of wet soil marking history with its savagery. The thunder of doors being kicked down, the tearing of clothes and shrieks of women as they were brutally raped and tortured by the soldiers, laughing hysterically. The carnage of that night stripped civilization of its humanity. Science had handed these devils the key to destruction.

The sound of laughter thundered against my skull. 'Stop it!' I shouted. But nobody heard me. I saw the skin and flesh falling away, leaving the skeletons. They surrounded me, reaching out with their bony fingers, laughing with their teeth exposed. They clawed at my clothes, at my skin. I screamed, 'Let me go.'

I shouldn't have slept with woollen inners. I woke up twisted inside my blanket, my clothes soaked through with sweat. I felt like I was being roasted on a furnace. My body was throbbing, my stomach was twitching. I ran into the washroom and spilled out the half-digested burek and Coca-Cola into the basin. I washed my face with warm water and laid down again. But sleep eluded me. The images from my dream still floated behind my eyelids. Leaving the bed, I pulled aside the window curtain and looked out. Did such a moon shine down on Novi Grad that day?

I trembled while bathing the next morning. I quickly had breakfast and reached the Modriča IPTF station at half past eight. The commander's briefing was over; everyone reported back to him about their previous day's work. I narrated my experience at the mass-grave site quite eloquently, but the commander was barely listening. Once I had finished my report, he told me, 'I am placing Mr Sharif on your team. He is our Egyptian monitor. He will help you.' Sharif came and stood beside me.

'Shall I write a report for you?' I stared at the station commander.

'No, it is not necessary today. It is Friday; I don't think anyone will read your report for the next two days. Give it to me on Monday. You better go to the Doboj Regional Office with Sharif and see to the forensic examination of yesterday's skeletons. They will give you the cause of death and the tentative date. But it will take about 10 days for proper identification. Go and start the process.'

'Should I report the development to you when I return?' I asked.

'No please, today is Friday; come back early and take a nap in the afternoon. Explore the popular nightclubs or the discotheques in the evening. It doesn't matter if you stay out late. You don't have to come to the station before noon tomorrow.'

He then pointed to Sharif, who was standing next to me, and said, 'This is your partner. He will take you to the right places at night.'

'Yes, of course,' Sharif said with a nod.

I looked at Sharif. He was of a medium height, with a well-built physique, an oval face and a large nose. He was clean-shaven with an almost military cut. I guessed that he would be in his early forties.

'Yes, Sharif knows the road to hell very well. Why are you sending this new boy to hellfire, what will you gain out of it?' Manzoor Hossain Changhaji, the Pakistani monitor, muttered in Urdu.

Sharif asked, 'Manzoor, did you say anything?'

'Not at all. I was only singing my national anthem.' Manzoor Hossain smiled politely.

'Your voice is hoarse.' Sharif grumbled. Manzoor, shrugged and left the room.

I shouted in Urdu, 'Brother Manzoor, don't worry! I will come back from the gates of hell; no incarnation can keep me there for long.'

'*Mashaallah, apko Urdu juban ata hai*? (My goodness, you know the Urdu language) Manzoor turned around and stared at me. Then, raising his hand, he said, '*Kal milenge, Inshaallah.* (Will meet you tomorrow).' He left the station with a smile on his face.

I peeked into the LA's room. Suzanne got up, 'Are you going somewhere, do you need any help?'

Sharif peeped in and said, 'No, beautiful, no need, I am going with him. I can explain to him as much as he needs.'

I went and stood outside the station. Sharif said, 'I am taking my car, you stay back.' Sharif walked to the parking lot and brought his car. I slid into the right seat. I checked my watch. It was nine o'clock.

Sharif eased the car out of parking, changed gear and accelerated out onto the road. He started speaking, 'Vettori is a bastard...' and other selective adjectives were the first words that came out of his mouth. Then, his jaw softened and he continued, 'We will be covering 40 kilometres. The road is snowy, but we should reach in an hour and a half. We will definitely return by two o'clock in the afternoon.'

I looked at him, wondering why he was in such a haste. He asked, 'What kind of girls do you like? Black hair or blonde hair, black- or brown-eyed. There aren't many blue-eyed beauties here, unless you are lucky. But I must admit, all the girls here have exquisite figures. Well, let me tell you one more thing, most blondes are dyed. If their body hair is golden, only then are they real blondes. However, if the girls here in Banja Luka...'

I cut him short, 'Sharif, why are you so interested in the girls here while I am worrying about our work?'

Sharif let out a low whistle. 'Does anyone come here to work? I have come to earn some money and enjoy the warmth of these *hurrie*s (girls of paradise). We have only one life, brother. Live a little. If I wanted to work, I could have stayed in Egypt. There is enough work in my homeland?'

Changing the topic, I asked him, 'I am very interested in your country, Egypt. I want to visit there someday. So many monuments, such profound history. I would love to visit them all.'

'Oh really? You want to go to Egypt? You are always welcome there. I'm a Cairo City Police officer. I'll conduct a guided tour for you. But Cairo is a very congested city; about eleven million people live there. Yet, there is no dearth of oxygen.'

As I stared at him, eagerly soaking in all the information, Sharif continued describing Egypt. He talked about many interesting incidents in Egypt, his eyes gleaming with joy and pride as he spoke of his country. Perhaps this sense of national pride is the same for all, no matter where they come from, especially when they are abroad.

Reaching Doboj, we took the elevator to the IPTF Regional Office on the ninth floor, to meet Tariq Khan, the head of Regional Human Rights. Tariq liked me immediately. I have been a simpleton all my life. But Tariq invented a dedicated officer in me. He asked me in Urdu if I knew the language. I nodded, but then said in English, 'But Sharif is also here. So, we should converse in English.'

Sharif nodded, 'Yes, of course, we should all speak in English.'

I explained to Tariq the purpose of our visit to Doboj.

Tariq said, 'You should have brought a written report on this issue.'

'The station commander prevented me from submitting the written report. He said that there was no such emergency before Monday. Is there any way I can send a report directly to your office?'

Tariq went into a tirade at my innocuous query. 'These people don't want to dig out the mass graves. Let bygones be bygones—this is their motto! I wish they would realize that even the dead have rights. Skeletons are irrefutable proof of their death. Their living relatives deserve to know that they are never coming home. Identification is not only for the next of kin but also to know their religions, so that they can finally be put to rest, following the appropriate rituals and customs.'

In between this impassioned speech, he opened a casket of dry fruits and nuts and offered them to us. Pouring water into the kettle, he then served us tea in tall mugs.

With a sip of the tea, Tariq said, 'This is an important incident. The news of the mass grave was initiated from our regional office, but we did not expect to find so many skeletons.' He gave us a form to fill up with a short description of the incident, which would allow them to start the forensic work post-haste.

He said, 'All the important work here requires the signature of one or the other officer from the international community. Without it, we won't be allowed to proceed. Vettori must have told you these things.'

'Vettori sent us here,' I spoke.

'Always send a report to my email directly. Vettori doesn't have to know. He is a white goat. Submit the report with the date to him. He will be forced to forward it. Does he do anything other than hanging out with Ukrainian girls?'

I was impressed by Tariq. I liked how he worked and the confidence with which he carried himself.

'I will send you the report on the mass grave excavation of Vukosavlje by tomorrow,' I said as I got up to leave. Tariq hugged me and mumbled softly, '*Bahoot dino ke baad apne watan se koi aaya hai* (After a long time, someone from my country has arrived)!' He patted my back and said that he would call me in case of an issue.

In the elevator, heading down to the forensic department on the seventh floor, Sharif murmured, 'There is no greater fear than the fear of death, isn't it?'

'True.' I looked at Sharif enquiringly.

He continued, 'Do you think Pakistan is scared of India? If you declare war against Pakistan, you will squash them like bugs, won't you?'

'Yes, they are afraid of India. Their size and resources are equivalent to that of a single state in our country. They cannot win, and they know it. But there are several Pakistanis who still consider themselves to be a part of undivided India. To them, India and Pakistan are like father and son who were separated after numerous quarrels.'

As soon as I entered the forensic department, my senses were assaulted by a rotten smell. But we were given face masks at the counter. The smell of cologne on them helped to keep the noxious odour at bay. I entered the office of the forensic expert and learned that the work was on hold for us. They asked me to fill up their form so that they can start with the work. Sharif took to translating for me.

'What is the process of identification? Will there be a DNA test?' I asked.

'Yes. But it will take fifteen days. Not all the reagents and dyes are available here. Many will come from Germany. The order has been placed,' said the forensic officer.

'Please let me know when the work starts. I would like to be in the laboratory for a couple of days, observing. I have never witnessed a DNA profiling before.'

The forensic expert seemed to hesitate.

'Is there a problem?' I asked.

'No, sir, thank you,' said another forensic expert, stepping in.

As we walked out of the forensic department, I turned to Sharif, 'Let's go to the court and meet the investigating judge so that the identification of the skeletons can be done quickly.'

'Why are you in such a hurry? Go another day. If you finish all the work quickly, they will pile more work on you.'

'I came here to work.'

'I say, get rid of the ghost of work, enjoy life!'

I got out of the UN building, walked to the parking lot and slipped into the car. Sharif pointed out the large park in the middle of the small city. I saw couples sitting on the benches there. For a moment, it reminded me of Victoria Memorial in Calcutta.

We went to the court to look for the investigating judge. A clerk came and accompanied us to his chambers. 'The judge is busy with a proceeding, but he has been informed of your arrival.'

The waiter placed two cups of coffee in front of us. The smell of coffee reminded me of the Vukosavlje police station and the skeletons. I left my cup untouched. After a while, the investigating judge came down and greeted us warmly. He said as soon as he got the green signal from the UN officers, he would start the investigation with the local police personnel.

I told the judge to draw up the paperwork. I could sign it if I came to Doboj or he could send it to me. The judge seemed happy. Sharif drove us back to Modriča. He dropped me off at my apartment at half past one and told me to eat and go to sleep. He would pick me up at seven o'clock in the evening.

Nine

In the afternoon, I went to the Modriča IPTF station premises. It was deserted. I completed the Vukosavlje report in a couple of hours. The first report was going to be submitted to the UN, so, I paid special attention to it. I decided to go through it again before emailing it to Tariq Khan. Saving the file, I shut down the computer. As I was leaving the station, I saw Andrea, the LA of the STOP team, entering the station, gnashing her teeth. Seeing me, she asked if I had seen Netherlands's monitor, Davis Renvier. Andrea was quite tall, so I had to crane my neck to look up at her. Her round eyes seemed to pop out under her eyebrows like the first bracket.

'I didn't see anyone at the station,' I answered.

Andrea seemed disappointed by my answer. She said, 'I went to his flat, he was not there. Not even at his friend's. Where did he go?'

'I've only been here two days. I don't know Davis!'

'Hey, that tall fellow like a palm tree, with white hair and a grumpy face like a koala,' Andrea described Davis. She peered at my face thoughtfully and asked, 'Whom are you dating today? Did you find your girlfriend?'

'No, I have arranged a night-out with Sharif.'

'Are you gay?'

'Hey, why would I be gay? Maybe I'll go to the disco with him, see where he goes!'

'Will you go to the nightclub with me, just think, if you like me, I can be your girlfriend too. Bastard Davis Renvier is avoiding me.'

'But building relationships with LAs on missions is strictly prohibited. Don't you know the rules of the UN?' I asked, startled.

Andrea rolled her eyes in frustration., 'Everyone says it, but nobody cares! Everyone has come here for fun and has the right to choose their girlfriends. How can the mission control our personal lives?'

From adolescence to youth, my romantic proposals had been dashed repeatedly. And here I was rejecting a proposal from a foreign lady!

Although I felt bad for rejecting Andrea, I knew in my gut that something was wrong. She seemed overly insistent that unless I took her out, the weekend would be ruined.

I was not eager to break the rules on my tenth day at the mission. I evaded her by disclosing that I don't consume liquor. She looked at me like I was from another planet entirely. I ran out of the station when I checked my watch. I was running late.

Sharif appeared at seven sharp. As I settled into his car, he asked if I had any objections with Srietlana joining us.

I was surprised for the second time that evening. 'I don't mind. But isn't there a restriction about taking civilians in UN cars?'

Sharif grimaced and said, 'There are too many laws. Who follows them all?'

Seeing that I was silent, he said, 'Srietlana has been my girlfriend for three months. She has been out with me every weekend. She is ready to jump into bed with me whenever I want. We hang out regularly. But she has expensive taste. I have gifted her a mobile and a second-hand Mercedes already.' Sharif smiled. 'But she smiles like Cleopatra with a dimple on her cheek. I guess, if we continue seeing each other, I will have no choice but to buy a separate flat downtown,' he said with a sigh.

As soon as Sharif whistled, Srietlana came out of the

house. Though she was an extraordinary natural beauty, her make-up amplified it. I don't remember the dress she wore. I only remember that she looked perfect.

Sharif started the car and told me, 'Pick up the local tongue quickly, and you'll get a girlfriend more beautiful than Srietlana. Girls will like your height and physique.'

I realized that they had already arranged the evening carefully. Srietlana flashed me a mesmerizing smile. Sharif eased the car out as soon as she got in the back seat. Her tantalizing perfume soon filled the car. Srietlana and Sharif started speaking in Bosnian. The entire atmosphere inside the car changed with the sound of her laughter and giggles. Her beauty was so overwhelming that I was forced me to keep my body twisted away from her, even though I was in the passenger seat.

After about 40 minutes, we reached a place called Šamac, on the bank of the Saba River. In her course, the Bosna merges with the river Saba. We flew like insects to the lights shimmering on the water. We parked our car under the embankment, with the other parked vehicles. I saw five big launches floating on the water. They were all decorated with bright lights for the winter.

Sharif put an arm around Sriletlana's waist as we walked into a nightclub called Hot Ice. He told me at the gate that they would meet me in the parked car around half past eleven. He winked at me and whispered, 'Enjoy this life to the fullest and when you come out, you shouldn't have any regrets.'

As soon as I pushed the glass door to enter, I emerged onto the dance floor, where the smell of alcohol and cigarettes suffocated me. In the midst of the dancing light, I spotted about thirty young men and women dancing to the beat of wild music. Even in such cold winter, there were hardly any clothes on the girls. Lots of leather jackets were hanging on the stands at the four corners. I felt suffocated. I peered at the faces of the people surrounding me and found an expression of unadulterated euphoria there.

Meanwhile, pushing through the crowd, two young women came forward to greet us. Sharif said something to them in the local language. Then, he walked towards the counter. I followed them. Looking at the two girls, Sharif said with a suggestive smile, 'These are Slazana and Amela. For a few dollars, I hope they will make you forget the sorrow of digging a mass grave. But don't give them more than 30 DM. Enjoy!' Then, he went inside with Srietlana.

Slazana stepped forward and handed me a glass of Coca-Cola from the counter. She gestured and said she would come back after a while. Taking a sip, I realized that the Coke had alcohol in it. I put the glass on the counter and looked at the floor. The rhythm of the music and the energy in the gyrating bodies of the people dancing on the floor was palpable. Even when drunk, they didn't miss a beat. After a while, Slazana came back. She took my hand and led me to the dance floor. But seeing that I was not a skilled performer, she stopped dancing and took me to a room.

A soft-pink light was shining in the room furnished with a single bed. Slazana gestured me to sit comfortably on the bed and left the room, closing the door behind her. I was wondering whether I should leave, when she returned with Amela. Slazana took off my leather jacket and pushed me to the bed, saying, 'Have fun!' Amela took off her dress and came forward wearing only her underwear. She stood close to me. Slazana gestured, 'Massage and hooking will cost only 40 DMs,' raising two fingers, she said, 'For two hours.'

I felt my heart pounding inside my chest. My throat was constricted, I couldn't breathe. I was sweating inside, and my body had gone rigid. The moment Amela pulled me close, a strong perfume invaded my nostrils. I sprang back in shock, pushing Amela away. In my distress, I shouted, 'I don't need this.' Shaking my head violently, I held Slazana's shoulder and said urgently, 'I don't want to have sex.' Amela got scared and backed away from me.

Distressed, Slazana pointed at Amela and enquired, 'Look what a beautiful figure. Why don't you like her? No one else is available now!'

I tried to explain over and over again through gestures that I simply did not need anyone. Slazana was stubborn. She thought that I did not like Amela.

So, finally, I took out a 20 DM from my wallet and handed it to Slazana. 'Thank you, this is your tip. But I don't need any of your services.' I said.

Slazana and Amela hugged me from both sides and planted two noisy kisses on my cheeks. Slazana brought me back my leather jacket, put it on and led me to a sofa nearby. She handed me a Coca-Cola and said, 'Sip it.'

I was out by the dance floor again. The sound, smoke, smell, lights and the people overwhelmed me. I ran out of the club within minutes.

I was alone on the deck in the flood of shining light. I looked at the sky, searching for the pole star. But the stars were hidden to my eyes, behind those bright lights. I looked at the horizon, where the houses stood like shadows, some hidden behind darker trees. The world slept in this unearthly silence, with thousands of mass graves at its core. Discarding the thought of returning to the nightclub, I decided to walk on the deck and go to the riverbank instead. I remembered that Sharif had handed me the car keys, in case I finished early. So, I decided to get into the car, start the engine and run the heater while I waited for them to return.

I pulled the chain of the leather jacket up to my neck, took a comforter out of my pocket, wrapped it around my head and covered my ears. As I walked down to the parking lot on the bank of the river, my thoughts lingered on the mass graves of Vukosavlje and Novi Grad. Who could have thought that a war-torn country, surrounded by foreign security, would celebrate a Friday night with such joy? I got in the car, swiped my driving licence in the control panel, turned on the engine and switched on the heater. Hot air poured into the car. After a long time, I breathed a sigh of relief. I turned on the tape recorder and inserted the cassette of my choice.

Enveloped in the scent of lavender and the snow falling like the feathers of a seagull, I don't know when I drifted off to sleep. I dreamt of Salim and Anarkali, Madhubala and nameless Bosnian beauties. As the Saira Banu I was romancing in my dream turned into Suzanne, I heard loud sounds of knocking.

Waking up with a start, I saw Sharif and Srietlana knocking hard on the car window.

They got into the car as soon as I opened the lock. Sharif said, 'How deep do you sleep? We were punching the glass furiously. Sorry, we're a little late.' I checked my watch, it was almost one and pouring outside. The car's cassette player was running *'Pyaar kiya to darna kya? Pyaar kiya koi chori nahi ki, chup chupke aanhe bharna kya?'*

Shaking in the winter, Sharif said, 'You Indians and Pakistanis are very fond of *'Pyaar kiya to darna kya'*. I have heard it a thousand times.' Focussing on my face, his expression changed. He said, 'Enjoy your life to the fullest, but it should not be visible on the face of a UN monitor.' Sharif pulled a paper napkin from the dashboard and handed it to me. I looked into the car's mirror and noticed the lipstick marks on my cheeks, the only thing that I took from Slazana and Amela. The scent of lavender vanished. Meanwhile, a drunk Srietlana had her arms around Sharif's neck, from the back seat. She was occasionally kissing his hairy neckline.

'You have to drive. I had too much to drink,' Sharif pleaded.

'Me?' My throat was parched. 'I can't drive this late at night, in such dangerous weather. Impossible,' I said.

'No, brother, you have to drive. I cannot drive in this condition. If necessary, swap my licence and drive. It'll be my responsibility in case of an accident. A least our lives will be saved if you drive.' Without waiting for my permission, Sharif stopped the car, swiped his licence card hung around his neck and restarted the car's engine.

As soon as I put my hand on the steering wheel, Srietlana grabbed Sharif by the neck and pulled him into the back seat. Ignoring their moans, I gritted my teeth and eased the car out of the parking lot.

Ten

It was about half past two when the car drove up to Drakomir's house. It was still snowing. Sharif and Srietlana had fallen asleep on one another. He groaned when I pushed him but was able to open his eyes. He said, 'Please help Srietlana to the house and put her to bed. She has the key to the main gate in her purse.'

I picked up Srietlana's purse and fished for the key uncomfortably when I remembered that I, too, had a key to the main door. I grabbed the key from my jacket pocket, went ahead, unlocked the main door and returned to the car.

I opened the back door of the car and nudged Srietlana several times, but she didn't wake up and fell back in the seat. I gingerly lifted her in my arms, and barely conscious, she started searching for my face to kiss. She was drunk out of her mind. I stood on the slippery ice in the middle of the night with a beautiful drunken girl in my arms, trying to wobble my way up to the front door, wondering what my grandmother would say if she would see me now.

Slim but tall, Srietlana was rather heavy. I walked into the house carrying her. I knew where her room was. Turning the latch, I pushed open the door to her room and put her down on the bed. She murmured something that I couldn't understand. Covering her with a blanket, I turned to exit her bedroom when Drakomir confronted me. Although I couldn't see his face in the dark, I realized that he was in a bad mood. I said, '*Ne mi, ne mi.* (Not me, not me).' I wanted to convey my innocence to Drakomir. Through gestures, I tried to explain to him, 'Sharif is in the car. I am going to drop him to his place.'

Drakomir crossed me by and entered the room. I breathed a sigh of relief. I got back in the car and took the driver's seat. I pulled up in front of Sharif's house. I nudged Sharif till he awoke from his drunken stupor. But I realized that he was in no condition to walk up to the second floor. So, I carried him on my back and deposited him outside his door, promising myself to never repeat this again.

Although I knew my office would open late, I still woke up at six in the morning. After freshening up, I returned to my bed and lay down under the covers, and recalled the events of the previous night. We were fortunate to not have met with an accident, and I thanked my lucky stars for letting me return home with my dignity. The thought of Sharif left a bitter taste in my mouth. I had thought that we would go to the nightclub and eat and drink together. At most, they would drink liquors and I would nestle a soft drink. Just then, my stomach growled audibly. I remembered that I didn't have dinner last night. I got out of bed and went to the window. As soon as I pushed aside the curtains, my room was awash with golden sunlight. Thus far, my stay in Bosnia had revealed the mercurial nature of the winters here. I had mostly experienced the cold cloudy sky interspersed with rain and snow. The drive to Vukosavlje was the first time that I had seen the sky so clear and blue. But the sun this morning was dazzling.

I moved away from the window and started preparing a hearty breakfast. I had never written a journal in my life. But I had promised myself that Bosnia would be a new beginning, and I would document it thoroughly. So, sitting at the table with my breakfast, I opened my journal, intent on writing down the events of the last eleven days.

I arrived at the station at half past ten. Our briefing room was teaming with monitors and LAs, but the atmosphere was quite tense. Something had happened before I got there. Seeing their grave faces, it was hard to believe that they had spent last night so recklessly. Commander Vettori was particularly busy; his face strained and serious. Vettori was walking around, shuffling a bunch of papers in his hands. I smiled at him when our eyes met, but he turned away.

The briefing started at exactly quarter to eleven. Vettori informed us that the deputy commissioner of IPTF had called him this morning and issued a much-classified statement. There was no progress in terms of work at this station; most of the monitors, including the station commander, were very careless and casual. Everyone was always busy with their own affairs; they spent their work hours frolicking with girls. So, he would visit the station for inspection next Monday morning. Raising the handwritten paper towards the monitors, Vettori said, 'Look at this inspection order.' The unit monitor alerted each team member, but I saw him staring at me on several occasions. Vettori avoided giving instructions to the Human Rights Unit, claiming that it was a fledgling unit. I mentioned the progress on the Vukosavlje mass grave excavation and what fruit my trip to Doboj had borne. Ignoring me, he said, 'I will forward it whenever you submit your report. Don't stress about it.' Seeing Vettori's reaction, I remembered what I had told Tariq Khan about Vettori. It occurred to me that Tariq might have complained to the MHQ about Vettori. I had said it light-heartedly, but Tariq must have blown it out of proportion and filed a complaint against Vettori. I decided to be more cautious about what I revealed to people in the future. I later heard from Suzanne that the commotion started on Friday afternoon and reached its climax on Saturday. Since Saturday morning, the monitors had been buzzing about a rather serious inspection. Everyone was busy on their computers, arranging their work. As I sat down at my unit's table. Suzanne handed me a cup of coffee and said, 'Be decisive with your first report and please don't make it too long. A British lady is coming for inspection—very squeamish, nothing can satisfy her.' Smiling mischievously, she said, 'You can see how Vettori's pants are turning yellow.'

I was shocked to hear such a crass expression coming from Suzanne. She noticed my expression and said, 'Don't panic, I know Indians are extremely diligent. Sometimes you write better English than the British. Call me if you need any help, I'm in the LA's room.' Suzanne patted my back and left my chamber. I looked at the report of the previous day, I didn't find anything wrong with it. I took a printout and went to the LA room in search of Suzanne. Handing it over to her, I said, 'Go through this and tell me what you think!'

With a twinkle in her eye, Suzanne hugged me, rubbed her cheek and asked, 'When did you make the report? Whenever a good report is written, it is written like a story. I like your observations. The whole incident can be visualized.'

At half past eleven on Monday morning, fifty-year-old Rachel arrived from Sarajevo. She reminded me of the widow Purnima pisi (aunt) from our neighbourhood. One after the other, Vettori began taking the work list. I presumed he was sweating even on this cold winter day. At two o'clock in the afternoon, she said, 'Lunch break. We'll resume at three o'clock.'

I went to a restaurant next door to eat with a few other people.

I got back to the station around quarter to three. The rest of them joined before three. Rachel returned a bit later. She told us, 'You go and sit in your respective unit; I will come to you, if necessary.' It was Vettori's turn to be grilled before the inspection team.

When Rachel came to me at five in the afternoon, she took my report and asked, 'Did you write this report?' I nodded. Without any further exchange, she took a copy of the report, put it in her file and moved to another unit. Her expression was inscrutable.

It was half past six in the evening when Rachel got out of the station and behind the wheel of her car. As soon as she drove away, I heard Vettori swear under his breath. Then, he called everyone into the hall, plastered an artificial smile on his face and said, 'Friends, I want to thank you all for your cooperation. Enjoy your time to the fullest.' The look on his face reminded me of the bandmaster Wallace Hartley from the sinking *Titanic*.

Eleven

An e-mail reached Vettori on Wednesday night, asking him to report to the Sarajevo MHQ by Thursday noon, for an enquiry against him. The LAs murmured, if found guilty, he would be repatriated to his home country. The German monitor, Liam Mueller, was expected to replace Vettori as the new station commander. As soon as I reached the Modriča station at eight o'clock on Thursday morning, I got the news from Suzanne. The initiation of enquiry against Vettori might have been a foregone conclusion, but the problem was that I, along with many others, had been placed as witness to prove the charges against him.

'My God, is that also mentioned in the e-mail?' I was shocked.

'No, it didn't say that, but I did find out from the personnel section of the headquarters. Gabby, I mean Gabriella Samarovich, the LA in that section, is a good friend. She told me over the phone.'

'That means I have to go to the MHQ and testify against him. Will Vettori cross-examine me on my statement?'

'There are so many details that I don't know. I don't even know the prevailing enquiry system.'

'Is there always such an enquiry?'

'Yeah! All that sounds pretty common to me. It's mostly used to tackle the unruly monitors. Moreover, it is included in the UN Code of Conduct. Many people are upto mischief, but only a few get caught. You could say Vettori's luck ran out. I'm sure it won't happen to you.' Changing the topic, Suzanne smiled and said, 'Andrea told me everything.'

'What did Andrea say?'

Without answering my question, Suzanne smiled broadly and entered the room reserved for the LAs. I tried to decipher Suzanne's suggestive smile but came up clueless.

Our briefing began at half past eight on Thursday, and the bell was rung by Vettori himself, 'Friends, my transfer order has arrived. I'm leaving today. Your new commander from the Sarajevo MHQ, Liam Mueller, will take over this afternoon. I wish you all the best, may your mission days be happy and successful. It has been my honour to lead such a wonderful team. Keep it up.' At the end, Vettori's voice trailed off. Everyone was standing in line as Vettori came forward, shaking hands and saying goodbye to everybody, one by one. Vettori came to me and stood for a moment, shook my hand and patting my back, he whispered, 'You have shown your class in two days!'

Was it appreciative or satirical?

Anyway, he did not offer an explanation. Neither did I. I did not think that Pakistani Pathan Tariq Khan would be so treacherous. I cursed myself for indulging in such frivolous gossip, which had now created such issues for Vettori.

Suzanne did say that list of charges against Vettori was long, but I didn't want to contribute to that list in any way.

I came back to my unit. Some complaints of human rights violations had been lodged at the station. Samer Hamidovich of despatch section handed over the papers to me. I went to Suzanne with the papers.

Suzanne looked through the papers and said, 'I can't translate so many complaints by today. But if you are willing to take a dictation, I can try to translate them for you right now.'

I had never taken a dictation before, so I told her, 'Translate it yourself as soon as you can. I'll wait.'

Guessing that I was distressed, Suzanne said, 'Okay, I'll do some of it at the earliest. You start work on those papers. I'll do the rest in the meantime.'

I was about to go for breakfast when Suzanne came out of the LA's room and lightly pushed my chest with both hands.

'What happened?'

Suzanne blinked and said, 'Let's go to the chamber.' So, I turned and marched back into my chamber and faced Suzanne, who came up behind me. I asked her, 'Tell me what happened?'

'Vettori's LA, Lilliana, was saying that Vettori was willing to pay you $500 to keep you from testifying against him.'

Surprised, I stared at Suzanne. I blurted out, 'What does that mean? He wants me to lie before the enquiry committee?'

'You don't have to lie; you can avoid telling the truth or misdirect.' She paused and said, 'Please take the money. It is a lot of money. We can have a good time for four weekends in luxurious nightclubs with that much, you know?'

Suzanne wants to go to nightclubs with me!

I said in a shy voice, 'Suzanne, I will not take any money from him. But if you want to go to nightclubs with me, I can take you with my own money.'

'Do you like me that much?' Suzanne asked, leaning forward, with both her hands on my table. Her big, brown-blue kohl-rimmed eyes looked at me eagerly. The two big rings on her ears swayed softly on both sides of her swan-like neck. Her eyes seemed wet. Shri Bibhishan Jana, my English teacher in twelfth grade, used to say that if you could read the body language of a girl, you would gain access to the gestures of the human mind.

My throat was dry. How could I tell this Bosnian Saira Banu that I liked her at first sight? I spoke in a voice calmer than I felt inside, 'Of course, I like your company! Who wouldn't?'

'Is that so?' Suzanne asked me in a husky voice.

I changed the subject, 'I will not take the money. But let Lilliana know that I do not want to harm or disrespect Vettori.'

'Okay. I'll let her know.' She moved away and left me wondering whether I had made a mistake.

Suffice to say, I had a bad day. I prepared a set of questionnaires for those who needed to be examined, choosing the events that led to the human rights violations. I noticed that Suzanne remained aloof all day. I returned to my flat a little before evening. Although I was not physically tired, my mind was exhausted. I was taking off my shoes and wondering what to make for dinner when I heard a knock on the door. 'Come in,' I shouted. Srietlana walked in. She was wearing a long gown and looked like an angel. As she walked towards me, I noticed that she looked upset. 'What happened?' I asked.

She stood in front of me, glaring. Using signs and gestures, Srietlana wanted to know what I did to her on Friday night. Why had I taken her in my arms? She was convinced that I had taken advantage of her while she was unconscious, that I had touched her inappropriately. I tried to explain to her that I had tried to wake her up in the car, but when she didn't, I had to carry her to her bed. And that I did the same for Sharif.

'If I was drunk, then why didn't you call my father from inside the house?'

'It was late at night and it was still snowing heavily outside,' I tried to convince her.

Without letting me finish, Srietlana shoved me hard. I lost my balance and fell back on the bed. I sprang up, and losing my temper, I cried out, 'You can't misbehave with me like this! Wait a bit, I will call Suzanne. I can't understand a word of what you are saying.' Something in my voice made Srietlana panic and leave my room. I thought she muttered something like 'Sorry'.

Srietlana's behaviour was quite unexpected. It was the last straw. The stress and sense of danger from earlier that day were spilling over. I decided to consult Suzanne at once. I got up from the bed, tied my shoelaces, flew down the stairs and out the front door. I searched everywhere, but there wasn't a single telephone booth in the vicinity. Then, I remembered that there are two phones at our station. Our Sanskrit teacher, Paramananda Mishra, used to repeatedly say, '*Krodham sarbdha paritajyam*', which means 'anger should always be abandoned'. But I tend to forget these words of wisdom every time I am angry.

I was the only one at the station. I called Suzanne and briefly told her about the incident. She replied in an almost nonchalant monotone that she would drop by my place tomorrow, before reporting at the IPTF station and talk to Srietlana. And with that, she hung up. I was disappointed by her reaction. I expected Suzanne to be a bit more empathetic.

I came back to my flat with a heavy heart. I got up to my apartment and decided to complain to Sharif about his girlfriend Srietlana. I had spent only an evening with them and now was being humiliated for it.

I changed my clothes, washed my hands and face, and laid down on the bed. Preoccupied with disturbing thoughts, I forgot to have my dinner. I woke up in the middle of the night with hunger pangs. I opened the fridge to get some eggs and saw a few sweetmeats wrapped in palm leaves with dried wood apple leaves and flower petals. Although half-awake, I recognized Dakshineswar's Kalimata's prasad given to me by Siddhartha. His mother had prayed at the temple for our well-being and success, and had sent that prasad to Delhi. I had ended up bringing it to Bosnia with me. Arriving at Modriča, I had kept it in the fridge with complete devotion. I tasted it and found it unspoilt. So, I popped five of the sweets in my mouth, one by one. On that night, hungry and sad, the sweets tasted like nectar in my mouth.

The sound of knocking on the door woke me up at eight in the morning. I laid in bed for a moment, unsure whether

I had indeed heard it. After the second knock, I opened it. Suzanne smiled and said, '*Dobar dan*, are you still sleeping?'

'I slept late last night,' I replied.

'Get ready. I'm calling Srietlana.'

After five minutes, Suzanne entered my room with Srietlana. Turning to me, she asked, 'What is your complaint?'

I briefly narrated how Srietlana had behaved with me last evening.

Suzanne immediately started translating it into their language. I noticed a change in the outline of Srietlana's face. I noticed their body language very carefully. It appeared that Suzanne was scolding her and Srietlana was listening quietly.

About five minutes later, Suzanne came back to me and said, 'Last Friday when you returned at midnight, her father was awake waiting for her. She is not offended by being carried in your arms, but due to that, her father realized that she was too drunk to walk. If you had woken her up and given her some time, she would have gotten up and walked on her own to enter the house.'

'How much time could I give her at half past two at night? I tried to wake her, several times, but she didn't respond. Yesterday, she alleged that I kissed her and touched her indecently. That's a lie.'

'She doesn't accept the allegation and is saying that you misinterpreted her for not understanding the local language. But she is apologizing to you for using coarse words.' After talking to her for a while, Suzanne told me again that she was really upset when her father refused to let her go to the nightclub this week. But I thought Suzanne was not being completely honest. Srietlana's body language was not the least bit apologetic.

I suspected that Suzanne was biased towards Srietlana.

After a while, when Srietlana left, Suzanne said, 'Get ready and come to the station soon. I am heading there now.'

I arrived at the station but couldn't concentrate on my work. I was dissatisfied with the way things had turned out. I was in the right, and yet, this did not feel like a win. My introspections helped me realize that my anger towards Srietlana had increased. But more importantly, my faith in Suzanne had been shaken.

Pakistani monitor Manzoor Hussain Changhaji started reciting Urdu shayeri as soon as we met. He asked very specific questions about where I lived in Hindustan, who I have at home, how much Urdu was spoken there, whether anyone in my family conversed in Urdu, and so on. He said that their ancestral home was near Kanishka Stupa in Peshawar, but he did not live there anymore. He had moved to Allamah Iqbal town in Lahore. But he missed Peshawar. History was scattered in the streets, lanes and bylanes of the capital of the former Kushan Empire. I promised him that one day, I would visit that city of Prithviraj Kapoor-Raj Kapoor-Dilip Kumar-Madhubala and splurge on biriyani made with cashew and pistachio.

Then he warned me against Sharif. He said that Sharif was a dangerous man and that no good would come out of our friendship. I remained silent so he continued, '*Kano kan khabar yeh hai ki janab bhi tasrib le gaye the isha wali mehfil mein*! (I found out through the grapevine that you visited the nightclub party).'

'Which Isha?' I asked, unable to understand.

'*Arre janab, ohi jisko angreji mein nightclub kahate hain.* (Dear Sir, the same place which is called nightclub in English).'

'Oh, the nightclub!' I smiled and said, 'I went, but I didn't do anything with Isha.'

'Remain scared for Allah! Be happy and mehfuz bhi!' Manzoor left the station, wishing me warmly.

There was enough time for the evening. I was going out to have a burek when Suzanne came into my chamber. She had translated most of the petitions.

'Can I leave office now if you have no assignment pending for today?' she asked me.

'I don't have any assignment now, you can go. But please arrange a new rented house for me as soon as possible. I will not live there anymore.'

Suzanne tried to say something but eventually decided against it. I did not insist either.

I woke up in the middle of the night to a sound. I was sleeping too comfortably to open my eyes, but I kept my ears strained for the sounds. Everything was quiet. I was drifting back into sleep when I felt someone standing near me in the dark. I could hear the sound of breathing. As soon as I opened my eyes, in the dim light of the night lamp, I saw Srietlana standing beside my bed, naked. It felt like a dream. In the soft light of the lamp, she looked like Venus, like the ones I had seen in the paintings of the masters. I couldn't take my eyes off her. My body was numb. She opened a side of the blanket and climbed into my bed. My arms embraced her of their own accord. The warmth of her body, as entrancing as it was, felt like a trap. *'If necessary, the enchanting woman can become deceitful at any moment,'* the warnings of my teacher Shri Bibhishan Jana ripped through my slumbering mind. I had taken a helplessly drunken Srietlana in my arms with honourable intentions. For all my help and honourable intentions, she had charged me with taking advantage of her and insulting her femininity. The warmth of her arms now felt like the clutches of a spider. I used all my strength to free myself from her embrace and jump out of bed.

Srietlana put a finger to her lips, beseeching me to not make a sound. She got out of bed and tried to hug me again. She folded her hands in front of her chest and looked at me coquettishly. 'Sorry,' she whispered. She repeatedly apologized and, I think, she wanted to say, 'Do not leave this house.' Suzanne must have told her that I was looking for another apartment so that Srietlana would not have another chance to insult me.

Srietlana seemed genuinely sorry, but I restrained myself. Getting involved in such a scandal while abroad wasn't worth the momentary pleasures that this woman was clearly willing to offer me. It could just as easily backfire. I showed her the door and then walked into the washroom to avoid her. I deliberately took more time than necessary, hoping that she would leave. When I came out, I found Srietlana standing there. On seeing my face, she picked up her nightgown from the table and left my room, muttering soft apologies that sounded sincere in the darkness of the night.

With a sigh of relief, I locked the door, got into bed and went back to sleep.

I was impressed by my own restraint and immediately decided to tell Suzanne about the incident so that Srietlana couldn't accuse me falsely in the future.

Twelve

I received an email next Monday instructing me to go to Sarajevo on Tuesday. I asked Suzanne to accompany me. She started dancing with joy, 'Will you take me to Sarajevo? Really?'

'Yes, of course.'

'I haven't been to my uncle's house in a while. I need to visit them. You know, my uncle was an army officer like my father, but much older. After retirement, he lives in a tower built for the army on Downtown Road, in Sarajevo. If you drop me off at the HHQ, I can take a taxi from there.'

'Okay,' I said.

I was a bit anxious about the enquiry. I wondered what the enquiring officers would want to know and what I would tell them. I wondered what Vettori's cross-examination would entail.

We entered the city of Sarajevo at half past eleven in the morning with such thoughts running through my mind. I asked Suzanne, 'Where is your uncle's apartment? I was told to come at twelve o'clock. We have reached before time. Come on, I'll drop you off.'

Suzanne clapped like a little girl, 'Great, I'm happy! I'll give you directions.'

So much joy for such a small favour.

Within ten minutes, I drove down the road to the Army Enclave. As soon as I took the car inside the gate, Suzanne said, 'Here, here! We have arrived.' She requested me to get out of the car for thirty seconds. I pulled the handbrake and got out.

Suzanne hugged me and touched my cheek. I said, 'I'll pick you up when I'm done. You don't need to take a taxi.' Once again, Suzanne danced with joy.

I asked, 'Memsaab, why you are so happy? Would you please tell me?'

'Of course. I'll tell you why, but not now.'

I headed back to the MHQ. The seventeen-storeyed building of the MHQ was housed in a huge compound. There were some plants, but they all wore white today. There was no way to recognize the cars, so each parking lot had a number written on the stand. I was told to go to the personnel section and wait for the report. If I had known that Tariq Khan would report Vettori on the basis of my casual comment and entrap me, I wouldn't have told him anything.

I decided that I was committed to the mission, and I didn't care what harm was done to one Russian monitor due to my statement. I would tell them the truth about Vettori.

I was waiting with a cappuccino in the chamber of the Deputy Commissioner (Personnel). After five minutes, Andrea came out of the room. I was surprised to see her. Was she also a witness? I wondered. She gave me a faint smile as she walked by.

The Deputy Commissioner came out and called me. As soon as I kept the cappuccino on the table and stood up, he told me, 'Please bring your coffee with you, otherwise you will have to take another one, and the mission will not pay for it.'

I smiled and picked up my coffee cup from the table.

Besides Vettori, there was an officer from Ghana in the enquiry room. The Deputy Commissioner introduced me to the Ghanaian officer. He was the fact-finder of this departmental enquiry.

'Hello, do you know that girl from Modriča station who just walked out?'

'Yes, she is Andrea.'

'Yes, Andrea. Was she trying to seduce you on Friday evening?'

I was taken aback by this line of questioning. I said calmly,

'She was not seducing me. She was simply requesting me to go to the nightclub with her.'

'Would you please elaborate about that?'

'I was working at the station until six o'clock on Friday when Andrea came in, looking for Dutch monitor Davis Renvier. She seemed rather distressed by his absence. So, she requested me to take her to the nightclub instead. I did not agree.'

'But was she trying too hard to get you to the nightclub? What exactly did she say? Was she pressurizing you to take her as your girlfriend?'

'She didn't force me so much as request it repeatedly. But I thought she was joking.'

'No, she was not,' the Deputy Commissioner insisted.

I couldn't understand the reason behind his insistence. Seeing that I was silent, the Ghanaian officer said, 'You didn't know, Vettori sent Andrea to seduce you?'

I was stunned. I glanced at Vettori. He had an inscrutable expression on his face. That was the first time I noticed that Vettori's eyes were light blue.

'No, I had no idea,' I said in a quiet, firm voice.

'How could you? Andrea gave a statement a few minutes ago.'

'Why?' I couldn't wait and asked.

'I think, Vettori wanted to turn the IPTF station into a Lovers' Den.'

I failed to comprehend this reason. I shrugged and said, 'I have no idea.'

'How could you know?' said the Ghanaian officer.

'You are right,' the Deputy Commissioner sighed. Turning to Vettori, he asked if he wanted to cross-examine me.

I looked at Vettori. He shook his head slowly, without looking at me.

'That will be all. You may leave,' the Deputy Commissioner said.

I took a last look at Vettori and left the chamber.

I had wrongly assumed that Tariq had reported against Vettori, based on the conversation we had had at his office. I had thought that Tariq bhai had betrayed me. Now I felt ashamed for thinking so poorly of the only other person in the mission who seemed to share my work ethics and a genuine desire to help. I also thanked my self-restraint and inhibitions that had prevented me from being seduced by Andrea.

As soon as I exited the elevator at the ground floor, I stumbled into Rachel Watts. I definitely did not expect her to recognize me, so I started walking in the opposite direction. But before I could gain more distance, someone put a hand on my shoulder. I turned back to see Rachel smiling at me, 'Don't you recognize me?'

'Oh, yes, Rachel, but I thought you wouldn't.'

'So, you were avoiding me?' Rachel's eyes softened into a kind smile. 'Come on, I was going for lunch. Join me, please. We'll talk while we eat.'

I was also going to the canteen, so there was no chance to avoid it.

'I will bring the coupons. Please have a seat,' I said.

Rachel ignored my proposal, forced me into a chair saying, 'This spot by the window is rather inviting. I'll bring the coupons from the counter.'

Rachel collected the coupons and brought her meal with her when she returned. Handing over a coupon to me, she said, 'Go and get some food.'

As I had woken up at daybreak and left the house after having coffee and boiled eggs, I was starving. I came back to our table with a big plate piled with food. I saw Rachel sitting there, her food untouched. As soon as I took my seat, she surprised me by saying, '*Bismillah karo.*' I was taken aback. I felt guilty for keeping her waiting.

I said, 'Sorry, had I known that you would wait for me, I would have returned sooner and taken a second trip to the buffet if necessary. Who knew you could speak Urdu!'

'Hey, it's not a problem at all. I live in Manchester; I have many Pakistani friends there. After serving the food on everyone's plate, we used to start eating together saying "*Bismillah*". I quite like this culture of Pakistanis.'

As she ate, Rachel revealed that Vettori had lost his ability to be in this mission. All the negative traits were already there in him from the beginning, but now they had been manifested. There was a long list of allegations against him, like provoking the STOP team to take bribe, getting shares from collected bribery, abusing the female colleagues, and so on.

She continued, 'He put an LA after you to uncover your weaknesses and blackmail you as needed. If he had that kind of leverage over you, you would never be able to protest against him.' Pausing for a moment, she said that Vettori's repatriation was just a matter of time, there would be an adverse report against him in their country. But most probably, there wouldn't be any punishment here.

After our lunch, Rachel led me to the gate, 'Come and meet me whenever you're at the MHQ.'

'Yes, surely.' I smiled and added.

I came back to the parking lot to find my car nearly buried under snow. I drove to the Army Enclave, where I had dropped Suzanne. Before I could wonder how I would find her there, she came downstairs, 'Let's introduce you to my uncle.'

I went up the elevator with her. The door to her uncle's flat was ajar. As soon as we entered, her maternal uncle came and hugged me. Suzanne said, 'Meet my uncle, his name is Ethan.'

Ethan almost didn't know English, so he couldn't say much, although he was extremely interested in me. Meanwhile, Suzanne was hugging him. I said, 'Suzanne, your uncle probably wants to say something to me. Would you offer to translate for him?'

'He talks only about the war. He sits and mutters and regrets about my cousin Miroslav, their only child. He has been missing for almost four years now. A twenty-four-year-old Miro went out to the market one evening and never returned. My uncle and aunt sit by the window every evening, waiting for him to come back. Rationally, we all know that it is too late now, but they still hope for a miracle.'

Suzanne went inside, I suspected, to hide her tears.

Ethan's eyes were also brimming with tears at the sound of his son's name. As I stood there, examining the lines of grief on Ethan's face, Suzanne returned with a plate. I looked into her eyes. They were light red. Handing over the plate, she said, 'Please eat, this is my auntie's *baklava*. They are like sweet pastry, with nuts and cream inside.'

I looked like a big barfi. I said with a smirk, 'I have already taken my lunch in the canteen, now stomach is full, forgive me.'

'Come on, eat at least one piece, otherwise my aunt will be heartbroken! I'm putting it in your mouth. You don't need to mess your hand.' Suzanne picked up a piece of baklava and held it close to my mouth. I had left my country a few thousand kilometres away, but human sentiments were the same throughout the world.

Suzanne said that even though they lost Miroslav, they still had Nadira. She was the best gift the war had offered them. She was named by Ethan.

Suzanne kept her hand on my shoulder and said, 'In 1994, Ethan brought a two-year-old child from a battlefield in Teshlić. Uncle was in the Second Line Combat Force. When they were returning from the operation, one early morning, he saw Nadira lying next to the body of her parents, crying, pulling at her mother. Uncle took her to the barracks and then brought her to the flat. Teshlić was a Muslim inhabited village. She probably belonged to a Muslim family. But now, she is their greatest reason to live. These two elderly people have sacrificed their lives for her upbringing.' After a pause, Suzanne added, 'Last year, Uncle officially adopted her. Nadira is that little girl who was peeping at you with big eyes when you entered the flat and then ran away. She is very shy.'

About an hour later, we left Downtown Street and drove to Cosmo Complex. 'I need to buy a few things. Won't take more than ten minutes,' I told Suzanne.

'Of course.'

We parked the car and got down. When we were collecting the trolley, the girl named Zinnia I had met earlier came forward. She smiled and said something to me. Suzanne was quite surprised. We stared at each other. Then they had a heated conversation in the local language. Fuming, Suzanne gestured her to leave. The girl shrugged and walked away.

Suzanne became quiet and grim.

'What happened? What did the girl say? Why did you quarrel with her?' I asked Suzanne.

Suzanne moved further away without answering my question. I went ahead and tried to stop her with a hand on her shoulder, 'What did the girl say?'

'You went to her apartment as a customer. I thought you were different!' Suzanne looked at me accusingly.

'I did no such thing. I didn't go anywhere with her. She must be mistaking me for somebody else.'

'You're lying, you recognized her, you smiled at her!'

'Oh, no! On my way to Modriča, remember, you were waiting to show me my rented apartment? That day, Labahari brought me here for shopping. I had been standing alone in a corner. That girl had approached me and said something in Bosnian, which I couldn't understand. Today I recognized her and smiled back.'

'Is that all?' Wait! I'll teach that woman a lesson!' Suzanne stormed out of the complex, looking for the girl, but she was nowhere to be found.

I heaved a sigh of relief, 'What did the girl say to make you so agitated?'

'She said nothing to me. Rather she told you, "I see you have got a good girl. Even if she is more beautiful than me, I could give you more pleasure in bed."'

My ears were burning. I looked down at my shoes, anywhere but at Suzanne.

I first bought a pair of flower-printed scarves for Suzanne. While I was picking up things from the shelf, I looked around and saw Suzanne picking up a few bottles of perfume and looking at the price on them. After checking out at the counter, I walked up to her and handed her the scarves.

'You took one scarf, you should have got only one,' she said.

'If I need flowers again, you have to donate a scarf, so I'm giving these in advance.'

She hung the scarves around her neck and said, 'Let's go.'

Just then I had an idea. I said, 'Wait. I've one more thing to buy.'

I ran and picked up the bottle of Christian Dior that Suzanne was looking at and returned to the counter.

Suzanne smiled when she saw the bottle in my hand, 'It's a girl's perfume, not for you.. Choose a different one.'

'No, that's what I'll use.' I looked at her with a smile on my face.

'It has just been launched. It is fantastic. But it's for girls. People will laugh at you if you use it.'

'Let them do whatever they like. You liked it so I bought it,' I replied.

Suzanne said nothing and remained silent.

Putting the shopping bag in the back seat, I got in the car.

As soon as I got out of the mall's parking lot and reached the main road, I handed Suzanne the bottle of perfume and said, 'This is for you.'

She took the bottle in her hand and looked at me surprised, 'Are you serious?'

'Serious about what?'

'Here, the boys propose with perfume and roses!' Suzanne cried out, almost agitated.

'In Calcutta, boys propose to girls with a ring, and that too, only after they have been dating for a while. I am giving it to you, but I am not proposing now. The day I'll propose, if I do propose, the white snow, too, will smell of this perfume.'

'Oh my God!' With a hand on her heart, Suzanne let out a sigh of relief. Only the immortal novelist Sarat Chandra Chattopadhyay could have described that expression accurately, '…as if huge monoliths were lifted from her chest.' She put the bottle of perfume on her lap, wrapped her arms around my neck and kissed my nose very softly.

'You see, my nose is naturally flat, if you kiss on it like this, it will become flattened with joy, so next time please plant a kiss in the proper place!'

Suzanne giggled. She bit my upper lip and looked at me with a mischievous smile, 'Did I bite in the right place?'

'Perfect!' I looked at her with a smile. She pulled away with a gentle smile and sprinkled a little perfume on her shirt. She asked, 'How does it smell?'

I sniffed for a moment and said, 'Fantastic.' This time, Suzanne closed her eyes and descended into the magic of the perfume.

Thirteen

As we drove, Suzanne babbled away in the background. I couldn't answer all her queries, but she was still buzzing non-stop. The car smelled of the heavenly perfume. Suzanne's kiss sent a shiver down my body. I asked her, 'You seem very happy today. Is there any special reason?'

'Yes, you could say that. My uncle and aunt always give me lovely gifts, every time I visit them. I always get excited to get my gift.'

'Have you received any gift this time? Where is it? I do not see anything.'

She grabbed a small box and showed a gold coin nestled inside it. She picked up the coin and handed it to me, 'This is from the time of Queen Elizabeth I. Look.'

'Is this what is making you so happy?'

'Actually, I love my uncle very much,' she said with a gentle smile. 'He was close to my mother. He wanted to adopt me after my mother died. But I couldn't leave my father all alone. But whenever I see him, he reminds me of my mother. They live in constant mental anguish. They cheer up when I visit,' Suzanne went quiet.

In the past few days, I had noticed that Suzanne was rather mercurial. Sometimes she would be a happy-go-lucky little girl, while at other times, she would be quietly melancholic. As if reflecting her mood, the sky too darkened at five o'clock. The shadows lengthened around me and the colour seeped out of the landscape. I realized it was about to snow. I became cautious. I had to reach our destination before the snow on the road froze over. After more than half an hour, the road became slippery, and I slowed down. Hail started to fall, as if someone was pouring sugar on us. The number of cars on the road became very scarce.

'We must stop or there could be an accident. I will tell you if I find a gas station or any other suitable shed.' After a while, she said, 'We are now only 2 kilometres away from Zenica IPTF station. Keep to the left.'

As soon as I heard the name of Zenica station, I thought of Siddhartha. 'A friend of mine is posted there. We had come together from Calcutta. He will be very happy to see me.'

'You go to the station first and find your friend's address. I am calling an acquaintance. He'll pick me up from the station,' she responded.

Within ten minutes, we reached Zenica IPTF station. I noticed that there were several monitors at the station, but Siddhartha was not there. When I tried looking for his address, a monitor came forward and asked me in Bangladeshi tone, '*Aapne Kolkatta theke aaichhen* (Have you come from Calcutta)?' He looked at me and said with a big smile, '*Aami oilam giya BBR Mani, pura naam Bake Billa Raushan Mani. Aapne aamare kebol Moni boillya daikte paren. Dhaha theikya challis kilometer dure ekkhan ganj aacche, naam Jamil Bagh, sehane aamar desher bari. Khaaran, aage aapner bandhure janai di je aapne ekkhan mem loiya aaichhen* (I am BBR Moni, full name is Bake Billa Raushan Moni. You can call me Moni. My native place is 40 kilometres from Dhaka, in a village called Jamil Bagh. Just wait, I have to inform your friend that you have arrived here with a foreigner lady).'

'Yes, I am from Calcutta,' I said. 'How do you know I am Bengali?'

'*Kanh ki Bengali deikhya chinum na? Jatoi estail mairya memsahib loiya ghuren khuni aapner mukh theikya maach-bhater chhaap jaibo kyamne* (No matter how much you roam around with a foreigner lady, how will you erase the impression of fish and rice from your face)?' Bake Billa said.

'This girl is my language assistant, Suzanne Grabovich. We went to Sarajevo for official work. But due to excessive snowfall, we are compelled to stop here for our safety.'

'*Aapne jatoi bolen emon gandha-maha jharjhare sundari aamago lage aaibo na* (Whatever you try to say, such a scented beauty would not prefer to dawdle with my type),' he replied.

Bake Billa called Siddhartha's house over the phone. He spoke to the landlord in perfect Bosnian and briefly arranged my dialogue with Siddhartha.

Siddhartha shouted with joy, 'Come to my place, immediately!'

'How will I go to your house unless I know the address? You come to the station first.'

Siddhartha arrived within ten minutes. I told Suzanne, 'Let's go to Siddhartha's house.'

When we were about to leave the station, Suzanne said, 'I'm not going. A friend of mine is coming right now. He's going to pick me up. I called him when we were making plans to stop in Zenica. He is about to come, but you may go with your friend.'

'How can I leave you like this? What if your friend can't make it due to the weather?' I mumbled the words as if there was no force in my throat.

'No, he will come; in fact, he is on the road,' Suzanne looked quite confident.

Within the span of our conversation, one hefty, about 6 feet tall youth arrived in a Mercedes. Suzanne briefly talked to that handsome man and said, 'Meet my friend Hamza Hedich.' Hamza grabbed my hand, saying hello. He said, 'I'm sorry, I'm in a hurry today, I'll talk to you later.'

Suzanne got into his car, and before leaving, said, 'Don't

worry about me, you go to Modriča as per your convenience, I will reach as per mine.'

I felt a little ache in my chest as I said goodbye to her.

'The snowfall seems to have subsided a little,' Moni said. '*Apanago Raj Kapoor ekkhan bhalo gaan likhyase ei sichuetione— "Bhramar khelailo phul, tare loiya gelon Raajkumar!!" Aapnare besh tukukhan hatash dekhaytese, Janab! Aamar lage bari loiya giya murgir surua khawamu-dupure tel-jhal diya raindhya rakhsi duma aalu diya. Garam bhater sange baraf-porah raiye murgir surua jomiya jaiybo ekkebare* (Your Raj Kapoor has written a good song for this Situation, 'Bumble bee helped the bud to sprout in full bloom, but the prince took away the flower!' You look a bit disappointed; so, I'll invite you to my home for a plate of chicken broth with rice. I have prepared that spicy broth with large slices of potato. On this snowy night, the spicy chicken broth with hot rice will be a perfect match, you know).'

Holding my hand, Moni pulled me with an intimate gesture. Siddhartha also said, 'Then let's go to Moni Bhai's house.' We picked up Moni in Siddhartha's car and went to his rented flat.

After we reached Moni's flat, he said, '*Aapne jama-kapod paltaiya lon, aami aapnare ekkhan lungi aar fotua dityashi; bathroom geyser chalanoi aase. Haat-paa dhuiya babu hoiya basen khuni* (Go change your clothes. I am giving you some fresh clothes. The geyser is running in the bathroom. Freshen up and come sit with me).'

'I'm uncomfortable in lungi, I think it will fall off at any time, don't you have pyjamas?'

'Yes, I have. But you are taller than me, you'll look like mullahs wearing my pyjamas.'

'That would still be better.'

'*Aare Bhai, lungi pora ekbaar abhyas koirya phyalaile ihar thikya comfortable dress aar nai. Aapneder Jyoti Basu barite lungi poirtye khub bhalobaistyen* (Hey brother, once you get into the habit of wearing a lungi, there is nothing more comfortable to wear around the house. Your Chief Minister Late Jyoti Basu, used to love wearing lungi at home)!'

The hot rice with chicken broth was delicious. I didn't think I had eaten anything tastier anywhere before. We chattered till midnight about the politics of Bosnia and Bangladesh, and songs from Rabindra Sangeet to Runa Laila to Sabina Yasmin were sung. The melody of folk music in Moni's tender voice is still ringing in my ears. Siddhartha left in the middle of the night.

Moni said, '*Raat koirya kaam nai, ghumaiya poren; kaal aabar sahale uththe hoibyo* (There is no need for further delay, please go to sleep. Tomorrow, you have to wake up early).'

I woke up in the morning and bid goodbye to Moni Bhai and left for Modriča.

Upon my return, I busied myself with work. Seeing the nightclubs from Friday night to Sunday evening, there was no way for one to guess how dark and gloomy the lives of Bosnian were, how much of their minds were engulfed by unidentified terror. Hundreds of unanswered questions; no information about their missing relatives; no meeting with loved ones for so long. When they talked to people in private, they could only sigh.

In the meantime, several mass graves were dug out under my supervision to uncover the history of the people in those graves, and no matter the cause of their deaths, they were, most often, heart-breaking. Most of them were brutally tortured and murdered for no apparent reason. There were various forms of tortures, many might say animalistic torture, but these incidents were incomparable with animal behaviour. It is extremely insulting to the animals to compare the act of killing people and burying them in mass graves with their nature. The instinct of animals is to satisfy their hunger according to their needs or to protect themselves. They don't have a religion, only instincts. Religion has been the bane of human civilization. Historically, it has always moved humans to inhumane cruelty.

Allegations of human rights violations began to surface in the name of local police personnel, government employees, municipal employees and even ministers. I had been working fast, with Suzanne's direct help in translating all the allegations into English, assisting in enquiries, writing reports, etc. Sometimes, Manzoor Hussain Changhaji joked about my workaholism. One day, a British monitor called Ian said, 'This is not your country, man. After a few months, you will not be here. Yet, how do you motivate yourself so much? You work like a crazy person all the time and don't enjoy your life.'

I laughed and said, 'I do not think in terms of my country or your country; the whole world is a country to me. Moreover, I am working for the people. Are the basic needs or the feelings of the people of different countries any different?'

One day, after finishing my office work, I returned home, as usual, at about seven in the evening. I had changed my clothes, washed my hands and face, and was standing on the terrace when Station Commander Liam Mueller came looking for me. 'I went to your previous house. I heard you were there only for fifteen days,' he said as I opened the door for him.

'Yes. This place seems to be more suitable to me, so I came here,' I replied, avoiding the real reason. There was some purpose to Liam's visit, but he didn't bring it up immediately. I asked, 'Will you have tea?'

'Yes, I can drink Indiski tea.' Our Indian tea was famous as Indiski tea. After making tea, I poured it in two mugs and handed one to Liam. As I sat there with the mug of tea, Liam said, 'Our STOP team will be raiding a farmhouse near Orašje tonight. From outside, it looks like a hotel. But it is a farmhouse. There are reports that several girls from Moldova have been brought to a hotel, with the promise of employment and are being sexually assaulted. They must be rescued and taken to the rescue shelter at Sarajevo MHQ. There, someone else will take charge of their safe custody. You will lead the team of raid and rescue operations on the farmhouse, for which I have separately obtained the permission of the IPTF Commissioner. You should have been informed earlier, but these things have to be kept confidential to avoid leaks.'

Liam picked up a copy of the Mission HQ order from his jacket pocket and handed it to me.

The police of the international community were reluctant for raids at night. But we were accustomed to night-time raids in West Bengal. In fact, we did 90 per cent of the police raids at night. I was happy to see the copy of the order where I had been made the team leader. I had two British monitors, and one each from Ghana, Belgium, Germany and Jordan.

Liam explained, 'You have to arrive at the Modriča station at two in the morning, get the rest of the monitors there, brief them and leave by half past two. That is your target tonight. The names and motives of the operation are not mentioned to the rest of the monitors who will accompany you. But since they are working in the STOP team, they must have guessed about the operation. The mission's intelligence branch reported that there are four guards with assault rifles and some illegal small arms. So, you need to be careful. You will have a German platoon SFOR with you. They will also report to you at the Modriča station. Two buses have been assigned to carry the victims and defendants of your operation, but those have been assigned to Smith Jones, the British monitor and captain of the STOP team. After the rescue, the STOP team will do the next routine work until the girls and the accused are put in separate vehicles.'

After finishing his tea, Liam left, but before leaving, he said, 'Best of luck, I wanted to lead this raid, but you got the responsibility.'

Fourteen

I fell asleep thinking about how the raid would go, with the alarm on the clock set to half past one in the night. For the first time since arriving in Bosnia, it seemed we had something in common with the work of the state police. At the sound of the alarm, I got up hurriedly and reached the station. I set off with the German SFOR force, and instructed the two empty buses to leave within an hour. I picked up an AK-47 from the armoury, with four magazines.

Within forty minutes, we were 300 metres away from the Derby Hotel. The psychedelic light of the hotel signboard was constantly spinning in the dark night sky. Our advantage was that there was a bend in the road. So, we could not be seen directly from the hotel. As per my instructions, two British STOP team monitors would enter the bar disguised as customers. They would want to see the girls and ask for more girls for bargaining. One of them would give us indication through torchlight signal.

As planned, British monitors Smith and Roy reached the bar-cum-hotel's reception. They had been in Bosnia for more than six months and could speak the language fluently. As soon as the receptionist opened the album for them, Smith said, 'I want to see real girls, show me at least five so I can choose.'

The receptionist got up and returned within five minutes with half-a-dozen girls, along with a huge Serbian guard. Roy came made an excuse that the money was kept with their cab driver and threw a torchlight signal at us. The hefty guard of the hotel sensed something was amiss, and pushing Smith out of the reception, he closed the door from inside.

The script partially went as previously planned. As soon as I got the signal, we forced our entry into the Derby Hotel complex. We saw Smith standing helplessly outside the main gate.

We got out of the car just two feet away. A few shots were fired from the side of the three-storeyed hotel. The bullets hit the top of the Nissan jeep of SFOR. I couldn't trace the source of firing in the dark. I ran back inside the car, lowered the glass window and shouted, 'Polisia.' They retaliated with few more gunshots. This time, the bullets missed. SFOR officers were also responding with their assault rifles. It was a fatal situation.

Bloodshed can never be a desirable conclusion to a rescue operation for foreign girls. In any case, I was strongly opposed to killing people, so I shouted at the German SFOR officers, 'Don't fire, sit in the car and shout through the window and give repeated warnings.'

'They answered with gunshots right before your eyes! Now we will shoot with the intention to kill those hooligans.'

'You may shoot, especially when they attacked us first. But, shooting and killing should not be the only option. What's the harm in putting a little effort to catch them alive? If you want to shoot in retaliation, please shoot aiming at the hotel parapet.'

'Is the parapet shooting at us?'

'Certainly not, but the warning will be strong, let them know we can shoot too.'

'Sorry, we will not shoot like this, we will shoot directly at the target.'

'This is my official order.'

'Let your official order go to hell.'

A few rounds of bullets were fired from the assault rifles. I think those bullets went through the air into the sky. That was exactly what I wanted.

At that moment, the lights went out within the hotel.

'We can run and reach up to the wall of the hotel, then taking cover from the wall, we'll surround the hotel. Stick to the plan,' I shouted.

I ran up against the wall of the hotel. When the others saw me, they followed the order and took cover near the wall. If the offenders now fired, the bullets would pierce the upper cornice. In any case, we were out of their line of fire. Now, everyone understood my strategy and some of them appreciated it. We surrounded the whole hotel compound in seven to eight minutes.

By this time daylight was spreading through the sky. The windows of the hotel were shut, and there was no way to understand what was going on inside.

We entered through the back door. German SFOR forces raised the rifles and covered the door. As soon as our presence was detected, a few girls started crying from inside. I patiently knocked on the door for a few minutes. When I realized that they were not going to open it, I had to tell the SFOR team to break it down. Suddenly, the door opened a little and the sound of crying grew more prominent. Opening the door with the barrel of the rifle, we entered the hotel room along with the SFOR officers. In the dim light, I saw at least a dozen girls sitting on several sofas in the big hall in front of us. Some of them were crying continuously. Smith went ahead and asked them something in the local language, but no one answered. I didn't think any of them understood Bosnian.

I asked in English, 'Where are you from?'

One girl pointed to three more girls and said in broken English, 'We four are Ukrainians, but don't know about the rest of the lot.'

A complete sweep of the room revealed a total of thirty-eight girls from the Derby Hotel along with twenty-one customers. Three hotel guards and their assault rifles were seized along with the ammunition. All three security guards were local residents, having gun licences but not for assault rifles. Smith asked in the local language, 'Why did you shoot?'

'We thought you were a Brčko gang of robbers, so we fired,' said one of the guards.

'You couldn't understand by looking at our uniforms that we are not robbers? What would happen if we were shot?'

One of the guards smiled sarcastically, 'You should have said that you had come to raid.'

Hotel owner Jibko Markovich was found in a luxurious room with a Bosnian girl. When we interrogated him, he said, 'I can't sleep without a girl, they are my sleeping pills.'

'We don't care if you take sleeping pills. You may take as many as you want. But why are you keeping so many girls in your hotel and promoting prostitution?'

'Me? What nonsense are you talking? Who told you this?' Jibko pretended to be surprised, then shook his head fervently and said, 'No, no, no, I don't, I don't do these things! There is a big misunderstanding. You have come to the wrong place. I didn't bring these girls here, they came voluntarily. I offered them a job, now whether they want to do the job or not, that is up to them. My door is always open, anyone can leave if they want to.'

Thirty girls were from Moldova and Ukraine, four from Poland, three from Macedonia and one from Montenegro. Each of them must have had a long history of torture and helplessness and stories of oppression in their past. Every one of them had fallen into the clutches of some pimp or the other and come to this war-torn country in search of a job. They must have been told that after the war many people gathered in this country with confirmed jobs. There was no way to talk to each of them due to the language barrier. Their stories of exploitation and harassment were later revealed through the interpreter.

Jibko said, 'Most of them were brought to me by a Ukrainian broker called Anatoly Kushner. If you want, you can talk to him over the phone. The rest came themselves by contacting local brokers to earn money. You can take them if you want and anyone of them can leave this job now. Everyone's money is paid instantly after her performance.'

Fifteen of the thirty-eight girls did not agree to leave the hotel or return home. They wanted to know how to regularize their passports and visas, and if we could come to their aid. I noticed a Moldovan girl who had been crying since we had entered the hotel. I tried a few times to find out the reason for her crying, but I couldn't because of the language barrier. Smith told me, 'I will try to find out more through an interpreter back at the station and let you know.'

It was about half past eight in the morning when we picked up twenty-one customers, the hotel owner and twenty-three girls from the hotel on the bus. I thanked every member of the STOP team, including SFOR. Everyone acknowledged that the decision of shooting would have been serious for us and though it could have been justified afterwards, that might have become a hindrance to addressing the actual problem.

After the operation, I came back home to take a bath and have breakfast. I reached the Modriča station by eleven o'clock. Liam hugged me when we met, and praised me for my patience and ability to handle the situation. He didn't realize how scared I was during the shoot-out at the hotel. Except the indiscriminate firings, in comparison to the police here, the police service in our country has more patience. Moreover, the daily disturbance there was hundred times more and full of diversity.

Suzanne came and hugged me, 'Your work has been immensely appreciated. I am proud of you. You said you would visit my home soon, but you couldn't manage time, no?'

'Oh! Sorry, it slipped my mind. I will visit your house soon, I promise.'

I entered my chamber and Andrea came to me. Without

any introduction, she directly said, 'I didn't want to lose my job, for that reason, I went before you during the enquiry at the instigation of Commander Vettori. But, honestly, I would never do you any harm or try to blackmail anybody. I don't think Vettori wanted to hurt you anyway. He wanted everyone at Modriča station to be as happy as he was. However, during his repatriation, his mission subsistence allowance was deducted by 50 per cent. It has been exaggerated by the mission. I'm sorry that I tried to trick you.'

'No, I didn't mind, but I sincerely thought you wanted to be my girlfriend.'

'Obviously, I wanted it. I still want to be your girlfriend. I've no relation with Davis now. He has his choice of girl,' Andrea said in a hard voice.

'Find a new friend too. It shouldn't be a big problem for a nice girl like you.'

'It is not so easy. Everyone is engaged now. Look, I told you, but you don't want to be my friend. You are deeply in love with Suzanne.'

'I have no objection to the first part of your words. However, I strongly object to the second part. How did you know that I'm in love with her?'

'Everyone knows from the way you praise Suzanne. Now, why are you denying that truth? If Suzanne hears this, she will be hurt.'

'I think you need to make a reassessment. Is it right to bear false ideas? I'll let you know if anything happens with Suzanne in the future.'

Pausing a while, she said, 'I went to seduce you on the instigation of Vettori. For that act, an enquiry has been started against me. I want you to save me from that case.'

'I heard you made a statement to the officers during Vettori's enquiry. How will you retreat from there? When Vettori's repatriation is completed, you wisely put all the blame on him. Clarify that if you didn't listen to him, your job would have been in trouble.'

'I want your help. You'll get what you ask from me because I don't want to lose my job at the UN. I'm a true blonde, but Suzanne is not.'

'You don't have to worry about me. You just have to deal with the problem of headquarters,' I replied.

Andrea left my chamber disappointed and that disheartened me.

As soon as she left, Suzanne entered my chamber. She had been entrusted with translating many of the complaints into English. One by one, she began to arrange the papers on my table and finally asked in a low voice, 'Why was Andrea taking my name?'

'Nothing,' I told a disappointed Suzanne and changed the topic. 'There is news of a mass grave on the bank of Saba River, in Bratunac, under Section 11A of the Orašje police station. Liam has asked me to go there tomorrow to attend to the excavation of the site. We need to report this at the earliest.' After a pause, I added, 'Talk to the local police station today. Tomorrow we'll go to the excavation site and then to Doboj. Orašje is just a few kilometres away from your house. If you can arrive at half past eight, then we can reach on time.'

Bypassing the issue of the mass grave, she repeated, 'Andrea was saying something about me! Why are you hiding that?'

'Sorry, there are no secrets to expose.'

Suzanne left my chamber fuming. No matter how angry she was, I was sure she would help during the grave dig the next day.

Fifteen

I wrote up the raid report of the STOP team as per the UN regulations and mailed it to Liam in the evening. After a while, he came into my chamber with a girl. I vaguely remembered her. Liam told me, 'Your report was correct. You probably asked Smith to enquire about this girl, so I brought her to you. Now tell me what you wanted to know?'

I recognized her as one of the girls rescued that morning. She was weeping incessantly since we had entered the hotel. The girl was a natural beauty. However, the runny make-up from the previous night marred her face. There was something different though. After changing her clothes, she now looked different, rather smart and intelligent.

I nodded and said, 'Yes, I was curious about this girl. She was crying continuously.'

'Yes, Smith told me. She is Anastasia Moraru from Laloveni. Her stepfather used to take her to the bar every day after lunch to pimp her till late into the evening. Then, he would make her dance all night. In the morning, he used to take her to his bed for his own enjoyment. To escape the misery, she fled to Poland with her drunkard lover, Raslan. They worked together at a Warsaw bar—Raslan as a bartender and she as a dar dancer. This lasted for a whole of six months. The bar owner rented them a house. Ever since her adolescence, Anastasia finally had started to enjoy and love her life. However, Raslan used to get into trouble with other employees at work. One such day, Raslan stabbed one of his colleagues during an argument. Anastasia was dancing at the bar at that time. Raslan was reported to the police. The bar owner told Anastasia to flee so that the police would not catch her. Inevitably, she fell into the clutches of a broker. We want to send her home, but she doesn't have a place to call home. What do you suggest? Where do we send her?' Liam looked at me questioningly.

'I hope you don't send her to Moldova's Laloveni. She can have job at the UN canteen in Sarajevo. Afterwards, she may search for any suitable job in this market, other than flesh trade.'

Liam looked at me, surprised. I said, 'If I had that power, I would have done it already.'

'Okay, so be it. Your recommendation will be shared with the MHQ.'

Anastasia looked me in the eye while leaving my office, and I could see there was genuine compassion there. Nightmares about Anastasia kept me awake that night. I woke up late the next morning. In a hurry, I got ready and started for Orašje. The municipality had cleared the snow-covered roads in the morning. I reached Šamac in thirty-five minutes. Earlier, when I had come to the Hot Ice Bar with Sharif and Srietlana, the bar was on a launch on the other side of the dam. I had to turn right at Šamac to take the road along the Saba River to reach Orašje. I missed my turning because my thoughts were busy with the location of the Hot Ice Bar. The car came to a screeching halt as I applied the brakes. At that time, of course, there was no one on the road, so I averted a major accident. I turned my car and continued to drive. On the other side of the Saba River lay Croatia's Babina Greda and Jupania. The road was lined with trees along snow-covered fields. It was like flying from country to country, like a solitary pelican, through a white blanketed landscape.

I reached Orašje police station in thirty-five minutes from Šamac. There were only two officers at the police station. I searched for Suzanne, but she hadn't arrived yet. I thought that maybe she was coming from her home in Prada. The police in-charge of the station was not there. He came in about half an hour later. As he realized my situation due to the absence of an interpreter, Samara, a middle-aged lady, was called for my help. She started chatting with me about herself to demonstrate her proficiency in English, which she had learnt in Brussels. At the age of eighteen, she had left for Brussels with a neighbourhood boy. But the boy's love subsided in a year, and he left Samara and went to the Netherlands. She got a job as a salesgirl at a chocolate shop in Grand Place and got involved with the owner, Alexander. As she grew older and her beauty faded, Alexander left her and she lost her job. Even though she said she had no regrets, her emotions while narrating the story portrayed a different picture. She never got married, and opened a departmental store with her savings. In a few days, she was planning to conduct a continental tour to the island of Hawaii in the US, and she was looking for the right partner to go on the trip with.

I told the police in-charge to wait for the others to arrive. I called Suzanne from the police station, but the call went unanswered. The police in-charge said that everyone else was reaching in a short while, and if we didn't leave on time, it would be late.

The police officer requested Samara to help me on my trip to Bratunac. However, she declined because there was no one to attend to her store and it would hamper her business. I called Suzanne again from the police station. She picked up the phone just as I was about to hang up.

'I didn't confirm for today. You could have taken any other LA.'

'If I had known you wouldn't come, I would have done that. I lost a lot of work.'

'You have to think about the loss of your work, right? Why are you blaming me?'

'Your decision to not come here today is a very irresponsible one. It is not my personal business. Both of us are working for the UN; it is wise to remember that.'

'You can report me if you want!'

I hung up the phone in annoyance.

The police in-charge gestured me to move forward.

As I was leaving the police station, I told him to join me in my car. We reached Bratunac within ten minutes. Everyone was waiting for our arrival to begin the excavation.

The ground revealed skeletons and skulls after a little bit of digging. Even though eleven skulls were found, one by one, their respective skeletons were not. The forensic expert pointed out that the bodies had been hacked to death and scattered across multiple graves. Not all the body parts were in this grave. I shivered at the thought of the atrocities performed by the attackers. There were a few houses that were a stone's throw away from the mass grave. The houses were at least ten years old, so nothing could have happened without the knowledge of the people who lived there. These people saw it happen before their very eyes, yet they were indifferent. Even after so many years, they did not report it to the police. A foreign reporter got wind of the situation and informed the authorities. Although we gathered there to dig graves, there were no local residents on the spot. Had Suzanne come with me, I would definitely have asked her about the indifference of the local people and would have tried to examine her facial expressions.

The excavation work was completed by half past two in the afternoon. Due to the language barrier, my questions remained unanswered. I wrote down the names and phone numbers of all the officers. I had to talk to them with an interpreter present before I could even dream of writing a report that night. Hunger was an afterthought. Saying goodbye to the judge, forensic expert, police in-charge and SFOR officers, I decided to pay Suzanne a visit. I got in my car and drove towards Šamac.

Sixteen

I arrived in Šamac at half past three. Suzanne had told me earlier that Šamac once had a large Muslim and Croat population. After the ethnic cleansing, most of the remaining inhabitants were Christian, but there was no way to tell who was a Christian or a Muslim by looking at them or their attires.

I parked my car on the side of the road and got down. I went to a bakery and bought some pastries for Suzanne. Next to it was a flower shop, which had a lot of beautiful red roses in the showcase. *Where did the roses come from in this land of ice?* At first, I thought I would buy a bunch of roses, but the price of one rose was 7.5 DM, which was about $3. I asked the salesgirl of the flower shop to wrap a single rose for me. As I was taking out the money from my pocket, I asked through sign language, assuming she would not understand English, 'Where are the roses from?'

She startled me by answering in English, 'These roses are not grown here. They are from a farmhouse in the Netherlands. Now, our country is covered with ice, so roses are not blooming. It is so expensive because I have to import these. Let the season come, I will give you two dozen roses at this price. We bring roses at such a high price because all men fall prey to this single passion: he wants to impress his beloved girl, be it winter or spring or summer or rain!'

The girl was talkative, so I asked her, 'Can you give me directions to Prada?'

She came down the road and showed me, 'Go another kilometre northwards from here, then turn west and keep going straight ahead. You'll see that the river Bosna has formed a loop by twisting itself; the village surrounding that loop is Prada.'

I was going to get in the car when the girl asked from behind, 'Whose house are you looking for in Prada?'

Looking back, I saw a mischievous smile on her face.

I replied with a smile, 'Suzanne Grobovich's house is my destination.'

'Go ahead, I already guessed a little! She is very beautiful and now she is not engaged too. Wish you good luck. However, their house is not exactly near the loop but at the end of the loop where a branch like an appendix of Bosna has come out. There is a two-storeyed house on its bank. There are a number of apple and cherry trees in front of their house, but you won't be able to spot them, as they are probably covered in snow.'

'Hey, I see you know Suzanne,' I said.

'I know her very well; we were students of the same subject in the same college, only she was two years senior to me.'

Saying thank you, I got in the car and drove off.

Within ten minutes, I crossed the Bosna loop and reached the Bosna appendix. But finding the house was very difficult. The main reason was not the language problem but the reluctance of the locals to interact with an outsider like me, particularly when the logo of the UN was prominently engraved on the side of my vehicle.

I finally reached Suzanne's house. Maybe she was near the window when she heard the sound of my car approaching, so before I could get out, she flung open the front door, ran up to me like a tide of the Kaushiki new moon and hung on my shoulder and said, 'My heart was telling me that you'd definitely come. I'm so sorry I was very rude with you yesterday!'

'Did you behave very decently even today itself? Will you let me know why you can't behave properly with me?'

Suzanne rolled her eyes a couple of times and said, 'I don't know really how it happened!'

I handed her the packet of pastries and the rose. She took the packet of pastries but not the rose. She mischievously said, 'I can take the rose only if you hand it over kneeling.'

'Hey, I'm not proposing to you. You are angry, so I'm trying to resolve your anger.' Then I borrowed the dialogue of a Hindi film and said, 'The rose is not actually red, its colour is pink, as it is also fuming like you, so it looks red.'

'Whether it is pink or red and you are proposing or not, I will take it only if you get down on your knees.'

Jhuta hi sahi, do din ke liye koi mujhe pyaar kar le— I remembered that famous song by Kishore Kumar. By that time, Suzanne's mother had come out on hearing the commotion. Suzanne told me, 'Meet my mother, Zainab Hedich.' Suzanne handed over the packet of pasties to her mother, who invited me inside.

Suzanne grabbed me by the neck and almost pulled me into the house, then whispered, 'Let's go upstairs to my room.'

As soon as we reached Suzanne's room, she pushed me on the bed, pressed against me and started kissing me passionately. After five minutes, she left me and said, 'You're not responding well, perhaps you don't love me!'

'No, I love you very much, but I have not decided about marriage. Probably it will be a mismatch. Your culture is very different from ours. Our country is different, not only in terms of lifestyle or food habits, but there are huge differences in social customs also.'

'You don't think about it. You know, my mother died when I was only six years old. A year after her death, my father fell in love with Zainab, whom you just met. He brought her to our house when I was only eight years old. Since then, my stepmother has been living in this house with her ex-husband's son, Suleiman. He was four years old at that time. Dad and

Mom would often quarrel, but I never saw their love fall short. My father was killed seven years ago, but my mother did not leave me. Suleiman is still here—as sensitive and protective of me as any other brother. Tomorrow you can chat with my mother and she will tell you how the two of them spent all these years together in spite of their completely different cultures.'

'You mean, I'll spend the night here, eh? Am I not going back to Modriča today? How is it possible to stay in your house at night? What will other people think, particularly your mother and brother?' I asked Suzanne.

'Yeah, you'll stay with me and nobody will think otherwise. They all know that I'm madly in love with you. You will like my company, I swear. You love history, no, and so we will spend the whole night talking. I have seen such a long civil war happening in front of my eyes,' said Suzanne with a sigh. 'You can't imagine the horrors and the weird things that have happened to me since 1992. I don't know how people transform themselves into worms of hell in the heat of the moment. But at the same time, I've seen some people who are as kind as Lord Jesus! What a strange human life. I'll tell you everything!'

'You have decided to settle in America. That is your dream. You must not have to settle in a poor country like India. We are Third World people. We still believe in ghosts, snake-charming and what-not. We believe in supernatural theories. No matter what we do, we talk a lot about religion. Our life revolves around religion, which is used as a tool to rule the country. People are divided in the name of religion, and the rulers of our country exploit this. Even after realizing all the deceptions, the mob becomes mesmerized like a snake in front of a snake charmer.'

'No matter what you say, I'm not leaving you today.' She got out of bed, opened the cupboard, took out her trousers and T-shirt and showed me to the washroom.

I had no idea that Suzanne was so serious. Even this morning,

I never thought I would visit Suzanne, rather my mind was full of the sights of the mass grave—the skeletal fragments of the human body in the grave, human limbs strewn like fish and meat pieces, continued to float in front of my eyes.

Suzanne's long, wide trousers and T-shirt fit me perfectly. We then moved to the glass-covered veranda and sat facing each other. Another winter evening was descending on snow-covered Prada.

Suzanne broke the silence, 'I was studying in college—in those days, when my father could not pick me up from college, he would sit on the veranda and wait for me to return in the evening. When I came back, he would ask me to sit with him in the veranda. We would talk about the happenings throughout the day. My father would tell me what vegetables he had grown in his garden or of the day's catch in the river. Dad loved growing vegetables in the fields and was addicted to fishing. He used to return home a little earlier in the evening after catching all kinds of fish in the river Bosna. On occasions, he used to tell me stories of the war. Even now, when I get home from work, I still think of Dad sitting on the porch waiting for me.

'On that unfortunate day, my father had dropped me off at college and promised me he'd pick me up. He was fishing when the assassins attacked from behind, I guess, as he had been in the army and always carried a large dagger and a pistol, so it would have been difficult to tackle him otherwise. The pistol and dagger are still missing. My father's murder remains undetected due to lack of witnesses.' Suzanne stopped and then added softly, 'We have stopped eating fish after Dad was killed.'

After a while, Suleiman came upstairs to inform us that dinner was ready. The three of us went downstairs together.

We had a dinner of chicken roast and bread. Suleiman came across as a smart boy. He wanted to move to Germany after completing his engineering degree and take up a job in a motor car company. But he would keep in touch with his mother and sister, no matter where in the world he settled.

After dinner, Zainab took us to her room, 'In this room we spent the eleven years of our marriage. The east wall and the cupboard are all mine and the west wall belongs to Joseph.'

I looked at the west wall, with a huge wooden crucified Jesus, and beneath it the smiling face of Joseph and countless other small and large pictures. There was a picture of Joseph in his Serbian army uniform with a fishing rod, and that of Suzanne, Zainab and Suleiman. I turned around and saw the east-side wall. That wall was rather plain, with cupboards all over the wall. A picture of Mecca was also there. There was a photograph of Medina, too, with the famous Mosque of Muhammad with the green dome and a tall minar. There were also pictures of Zainab, at various ages. Beautifully arranged glassware was displayed in the shelves of one of the glass cupboards.

After talking for a long time, we got up to go to bed.

Just then, Suzanne's cell phone rang, and it was Liam on the other side. He was looking for me, and since I didn't have a cell phone with me, he thought Suzanne would be with me. Suzanne handed over the phone to me.

Liam informed me that Anastasia had died by suicide and asked me to reach Mordica station immediately. After we had rescued her from the Derby Hotel, she was placed in a safe home with the other girls. They were to wait there for the final decision from the MHQ for their rehabilitation or repatriation. The girl had not eaten anything all day. In the evening, she was found hanging from the shower stand in the bathroom.

I had to go back and record the statement of the other girls staying with her, as they were due to be shifted to another place the next day. So, it was very important to record the statements of the other girls that night itself.

'Okay, I'm coming.' I left the phone and went to Suzanne's room to get dressed.

'I will come with you!' said Suzanne, coming into the room.

The two of us got into the car and drove off quickly. It was half past eleven.

Anastasia's death shook me to my core. She would have survived if I had not rescued her from the Derby Hotel. The atheist believes that death is the end of all. However, those who believe in God believe in rebirth. I don't believe in reincarnation. People end their earthly journey with death. Science also says so, and I am always with science.

Seventeen

January and February passed by in a monotonous manner. One afternoon at a tea party in Modriča station in the first week of March, some European monitors asked me, 'Will you Indians return to the country, with mass-scale genocide underway in Gujarat?'

I said, 'India is a huge country. This is happening in one of its 27 states. Our country will take care of it.'

'So many people have been murdered and properties looted in the name of religion. Pregnant girls are being raped and babies are being killed, while you have come here to ensure peace in a foreign country?' British monitor David Cork asked as he wiped his glasses.

I bowed my head in shame. I was trying to deliver a befitting answer. I said with a smirk, 'You see, everything will be fine in due course!'

David didn't stop at that. He was changing channel after channel with the TV remote in his hand. 'Look at the BBC or Vox! Everyone is showing the news. It is really sad to see that you have not gone back yet. You are here in the lure of a handful of dollars. You insult the British because we ruled your country. Now you can't run your own country! Go home, go and see the pride of your civilization burning and in the skies of Ahmedabad.'

'Your country perpetrated many atrocities in our country for two centuries. Your people have committed atrocities like the Jallianwalla Bagh massacre; hanged hundreds of revolutionaries. Stories of such atrocities are still fresh in our memory. How dare you criticize our country?' I replied in a challenging tone.

'No, no, no, please listen to me! No matter what the rulers of our country did, they never jailed or hanged anyone without a fair trial. I can swear to this with confidence.'

'Who are you to judge the people of our country? And how can you justify the misdeeds of your forefathers against our ancestors?' I answered, making eye contact with David.

Sensing an altercation between the two of us, the Nigerian monitor Abhichav Boye stood up and shouted, 'Calm down, calm down, please calm down! Let all of us go to my place. I have made soup with calf head and I invite you all to taste it.' Though calm in nature, Abhichav weighed 118 kilograms and was 6'6", so his appearance was in contrast to his temperament. This time he said very sincerely, 'Please come to my house without quarrelling! I think I can entertain you properly.'

'I'm going to eat your soup,' said the Egyptian monitor.

Labahari put his hand on my shoulder and said in Hindi, '*Chhod do, yaar, yahan gore log zyada hai* (Leave it, Buddy, there are too many White people here).'

Gerald, one of the German monitors of the peacekeeping force, smiled and pushed everyone away, and the chatter broke down.

I drove back to my rented house and turned on the TV. The German channel Vox was also showing the news of Gujarat. It started on 27 February at the Godhra Railway station, with the burning of fifty-six kar sevaks returning to Ayodhya. One after another, people were being killed. People were being burnt alive, along with rampant looting and raping. Houses, shops and markets were set ablaze too, but the violence wouldn't stop. One by one, the news of Gulberg Society's murder, the Naroda Patiya massacre and a few other incidents from different parts of Gujarat were flashing on the TV. The Gujarat sky was filled with black smoke and the wails of the distressed people.

Even sititng in Europe, I got the distinct feeling that we were sinking into the abyss of an unknown sea of hatred-violence-revenge in the name of religion.

∽

Meanwhile, there was no sign of the winter receding. Intermittent snowfall triggered my mental fatigue. This was the first time I felt completely exhausted. I wondered what I was doing in this foreign land, away from relatives and friends. *Was it just for the few extra dollars?* We had to read European history before joining the UN mission. When I learnt about the ethnic cleansing in the civil-war-torn Bosnia, I couldn't stop drawing parallels with the exodus of Kashmiri Pandits from the Kashmir valley in the early 1990s. Above all, stories of the Srebrenica massacre shook my whole being. I made up my mind to go to Srebrenica at least once. On the second Friday in March, I approached Suzanne to take me there. 'If you listen to the recent story of Srebrenica, you might think you're listening to a story from medieval era, however, it happened only in the last decade of the twentieth century. It would have been nice to go there in the summer, but you can still go. It's in the south-east, with Serbia on the other side of the Drina River in the eastern side. Since it is much drier now, Srebrenica does not get much snowfall. It is about 200 kilometres from here and takes about four hours to get there. If we leave in the morning, we can return by nightfall,' Suzanne informed me.

On the fateful day of 13 July 1995, when we were watching Madhuri Dixit cast her spell with the song *'Ankhiya milao kabhi ankhiya churao, kya tune kiya jadu'* at the evening show in a movie theatre in Calcutta, the crystal-clear water of Drina River was red with the blood of Bosnian people.

After office hours on Saturday evening, Suzanne and I finalized our plans for our trip the next day. I would pick her up from Šamac and from there head to Srebrenica through Brčko.

I woke up on Sunday morning and drove to the gas station. Luckily, the sun was shining brightly that day and there was no snow on the road. I reached Šamac in thirty-five minutes. I found Suzanne waiting for me at the appointed crossing on the road to Šamac. She got in the car, hugged me and touched my cheek. We were driving along the bank of the river Saba towards Orašje. We reached Bratunac in twenty minutes, and I pointed out to the mass grave that was dug the day I went to meet her, 'Do you know, the assassins had cut and buried eleven people here? The local people here saw everything with their own eyes but did not protest or even inform anyone. The day we came to dig the grave, no one cooperated at all.'

'It is nothing!' Suzanne said with a little contempt. 'Think of where we are going, eight thousand five hundred people were eliminated in two days! How many graves will you dig? What else can be found by digging graves? There are graves all over Bosnia. Will those people come back again?' Suzanne asked me.

'No, those people will never come back. But we just want to keep a record, show a little respect, and offer reassurance and comfort to their near and dear ones.'

'If the old wound is pierced, hatred may grow, then who will benefit? The people of the house no longer want to dig graves for further grief, neither will they return and nor anyone will be found. People are slowly beginning to accept their loss. Now they are looking ahead and moving forward with what they have.'

'You are partially correct, but everything needs to be accounted for. Transparency is very important in documenting history. People will learn from history and will not repeat the folly easily,' I said in the manner of a philosopher.

'Then why did your country not learn? What is happening in your country? Has there not been an incident like Gujarat in your country in the recent past? Was not ethnic cleansing contemplated there? So many instances are there, something similar, even if not on the same scale. Moreover, will each country learn only from the events of their own country? Will they not learn a lesson from the history of another country? Why would this happen in the twenty-first century, when we have enough history to learn from?'

I had no answer to this question.

We passed Orašje after some time. 'I felt very bad when you didn't come to Orašje that day. I lost my temper.'

Suzanne was silent for a moment, let out a long sigh and said, 'I'll make up for the loss of work. Just think how close we came that day, only because you felt bad. If Anastasia hadn't died by suicide that night, we would have…'

'It's best we didn't go that far. We shouldn't do anything hastily. There are so many issues to resolve among ourselves…' I whispered in a low note.

'Are all the issues of life always resolved? If some issues are not resolved, does life come to a standstill?' she asked, looking straight at me.

Just then I spotted a fast-food counter on the side of the road and stopped the car. I got down and walked up to the counter. I got us our usual—burek, sandwiches and Coca-Cola.

'Hey, have we reached Brčko so soon?' Suzanne called out to me from the car. 'Look at how this Brčko district was divided, including Brčko Town—48 per cent of the land belongs to Republika Srpska (Republic of Serbia) and the remaining 52 per cent to Bosnia. Is it possible to divide vegetable fields, cities, habitats, rivers and hills in this way? Warlords will one day want to divide the air. People and domesticated animals can be divided. But I don't know how birds and wild animals will be divided.'

Back in the car, I said, 'You're right. Maybe one day people will do just that. Countries around the world waste trillions of dollars just protecting their borders. If people could unite and accept nonaggression as the way forward, then all that money spent in war could be spent on education and development throughout the world.'

'Take the right. I have a faint idea of the road. I was here four years ago, so I don't exactly remember.' Pausing for a moment, Suzanne said, 'We'll go to Bratunac first and then to Bratunac. You need to visit this Bratunac town. From Bratunac, it is just 10–12 kilometres to Srebrenica.'

The car was running fast and Suzanne was humming and singing. The melody was very beautiful, but I didn't understand the lyrics of the song. I asked her, 'Are you singing?'

'Hey, it's a very old song—"I Only Have Eyes For You," by the Flamingos. Tommy Hunt was the lead singer. This song had been sung by many since then and used in several movies.'

We reached Bratunac in a short while. At noon, we got out of the car and stood on the Bratunac field in the valley of the river Drina. It was cloudy and breezy. Suzanne said, 'Thousands of Bosnian people were brought to the field from the Potočari jungle. On the night of 11 July 1995, they left Srebrenica to flee to the jungle, but were asked to surrender with false promises of their safety. It was here that the girls and women were separated, lined up and sent to army camps in buses brought from Serbia.'

I looked around. The landscape comprised small hills and dense vegetation covered with ice. 'Is this the biggest wound of ethnic cleansing?' I asked myself.

Suzanne could have read my thoughts, 'Not only here, but in the whole of Srebrenica and its surrounding areas. The riots continued till 16 July. After the surrender, many men and boys were brought from different areas to Bratunac and kept in different camps. From there, they were taken to Vlasenica and Nova Kasaba, Kravica, Karakaj, Orahovac schools, the Cerska Valley, the Cultural

Centre of Pilica, and to many other such shelters.'

'Who was leading this hellish torment?' I asked.

'Who else can it be? That cannibal, Group Commander Radislav Krstić. On the field, Vujadin Popovic and Ljubiša Beara led the killings. How many names do I mention? There were so many senior Serbian army officers involved in the heinous crime.' After a moment of silence, Suzanne said that on 11 July, the kingpin of the Serb military, Ratko Mladić, arrived in Srebrenica. He started the campaign against the Muslim community.

My head started spinning thinking of how thousands of helpless people once stood where I was standing that day! After surrendering, they knew they would be killed or shot dead shortly afterwards. I didn't have the ability to even imagine the state of mind of those helpless people.

Suzanne said, 'Let's get in the car and go a little further up the riverbank.'

I drove east of the Bratunac Municipality to the banks of the Drina. I got out of the car and walked up to the riverbank. Suzanne and I sat side by side on a large rock. On the other side of the river was another country, Serbia.

The blood of thousands of people was blended in the water of this river that day. I got up from the rock, took off my gloves and dipped my hands in the ice-cold water. I felt the warmth of human blood in it.

Suzanne was staring at the water. I looked at her and said in a low voice, 'There are thousands of people buried in the crevices of the hillocks on both sides of this river. Their bodies were brought in garbage trucks and dumped there. The girls were not spared even after rape and physical torture. Many girls' nipples were bitten off by the valiant warriors. What a boast of heroism!'

How would I introduce myself as a human being after these soldiers brought so much shame on mankind? I wondered.

Seeing me silent, Suzanne said, 'Let's go to Srebrenica.'

Eighteen

After driving for some twenty minutes, Suzanne whispered, 'This is Srebrenica. The people here call it Srebrenista, meaning "silver mine". Once upon a time, there was a real mine here, now everything is closed. About thirty thousand people who fled as a result of ethnic cleansing have not returned yet. No one knows when they will return or whether they will return at all.'

We were driving along the road flanked by steep hills on both sides. Quite uncharacteristically, Suzanne was completely silent.

We then drove up to an elongated lake, actually a small pond at the foot of the hill. Suzanne said, 'Stop the car here.'

I stopped the car, and we went up to the lake. It had very clear water, but there was no current.

There were some houses scattered far and wide. Several houses had a dilapidated look, while some looked like they had been repaired.

Looking at the small town at a glance, Suzanne said, 'People here have become like robots now. If you ask something, you will not get an answer. They do not talk about war. Let's go for a walk.'

I looked all around while walking behind Suzanne. The houses, like the other small municipalities in Bosnia, were a short distance apart, not like our houses in congested habitations. Even during the day, the road was almost empty. But I wanted to talk to the people there.

There were a couple of small mosques near the crossroads. A little further across, and after a few houses, there was also a small church. My eyes kept searching for people. A middle-aged woman was sitting in a small grocery store. I walked over to her, waved my hand and bought two chocolates. Suzanne asked the woman her name, to which she replied in her language. Naturally, I couldn't understand anything. When I turned towards her to give her the chocolate, I saw Suzanne turn pale. She thanked me, and taking the chocolate in her hand, said, '"When your boyfriend is offering you chocolate, eat it. What will you do knowing my name?"' That was the woman's answer to my question.

Walking back to the car, we saw a young man and a kid on a bicycle. There was no way to tell if they were Serbian or Bosnian. 'Once upon a time this village was vibrant with life. But now there are very few people living here. About forty thousand people lived here earlier. And today, there must be hardly two thousand people here. Most of the houses are still in a dilapidated and burnt condition. The Bosnian Muslim survivors who fled have not been able to recover from the trauma yet. While the Serbs, for whom the Serbian army perpetrated the atrocities, are no longer living here. I don't know when normalcy will be restored to this cursed place!' Suzanne let out a heavy sigh.

'Can we just sit on the edge of the lake?' I looked at Suzanne.

'Yes, let's go.' Walking back to the shore of the lake, we saw a huge, clear rock and sat on it, side by side.

'Would you like a sandwich?' Suzanne looked at me.

'No, you may eat if you wish, I won't.'

Suzanne seemed hungry, but she didn't move. Her eyes were closed, as if she was travelling through time. Then she said with a long sigh, 'Since 1992, the aim of Serbs in Bosnia was to acquire Srebrenica. The dream was elusive because Srebrenica was a Muslim-majority area, and they had no aspiration to be merged with the Republika Srpska. In 1995, Serbian President Radovan Karadžić added fuel to the fire. At his behest, the persecution of the Bosnians began, forcing them to leave their homes and Srebrenica too. The complete economic blockade was started by the order of the self-proclaimed president. He stopped the supply of food and other necessities. Meanwhile, in 1993, the United Nations Security Council declared Srebrenica a Safe Zone. The Bosnian Muslims refused to leave Srebrenica, relying on the UN. Seeing no positive results from the economic blockade, the desperate Serbian army made a perfect plan to capture Srebrenica. Drastic action was taken against the Muslims in the name of the special operation called Krivaya 95. From the first week of July, as planned, the Serbian army's Scorpion Command stormed into Srebrenica, escalating the persecution of Bosnians several times by burning houses, firing indiscriminately and selectively killing people. Many Bosnians fled from the area, but still about twenty-five thousand people remained in their homeland, which was more than half of the total population of forty thousand. Eventually, extreme measures were executed against them through ethnic cleansing. UN Secretary-General Kofi Annan later called the Srebrenica incident a genocide. The International Criminal Tribunal for the former Yugoslavia (ICTY) also used the same term against the mass killings.'

Suzanne sat quietly. After maintaining silence for a long time, she said, 'Let's go back now.'

As I approached the car parked on the shore of the lake, I asked if the Scorpion Command had disposed of any dead body in the lake at that time.

'No, as far as I've heard. No dead body was dropped or buried in the lake or on the side of the road. The Serbs wanted to live here. Therefore, they didn't want to disgrace or malign the area. Look how beautiful this place is. Like a divine picture. It is snowy here, but not as snowy as other places in Bosnia. Some plants here are green even in winter.'

We had started when the sun was shining brightly, but now in the afternoon, it had disappeared.

'Let's start, otherwise we will be late,' Suzanne said, getting up on her feet. We walked up to the car, hand in hand. 'Thank you so much, Suzanne, for bringing me here. One of the worst crimes in the modern world took place in this valley. I'll be back in the summer again. If possible, on 13 July, will you come?' I looked at Suzanne for her approval. Suzanne nodded silently.

I thought to myself: can't we learn from this genocide in Srebrenica? ICTY announced life imprisonment against Mladić in 2017 for heinous crime against humanity and mankind. He has been serving prison sentence.

ꝏ

On the Friday morning in the last week of March, when the briefing was over, Commander Liam called me and said, 'Many monitors are being repatriated in a day or two, as their terms are coming to an end, so the MHQ is relocating the existing monitors. You don't have to work in Modriča anymore.' Extending his right hand, Liam said, 'Congratulations, you have been appointed as the Regional Human Rights Officer in Doboj for your next assignment.'

I shook hands with Liam and asked, 'Isn't one Tariq Khan of Pakistan Police Service presently holding that post?'

'Yeah, that's right! But as his repatriation is scheduled for next month, he has shifted to Sarajevo MHQ, and you have been posted in his place. You better go to Doboj tomorrow, see your office and at the same time search for a suitable accommodation for yourself.'

'I have seen that office several times!' I replied.

I dreaded packing up my suitcases again and moving to a new place. I called my friend Siddhartha in Zenica and informed him the same. He was delighted to announce that he would also be joining the SRU (Special Response Unit) in Doboj next week. Initially, I was very upset after receiving the transfer order, but when I heard that Siddhartha would also be in Dojob, I found some comfort in it.

By the end of the day, I sorted out all my pending jobs. There were some reports left. I re-endorsed them for my successor and returned them to the station commander. Suzanne hugged me with tears in her eyes, 'Will you leave Modriča forever? I have been working with many officers from many countries for the last four years, but I have never seen such a sincere person like you with so much love for the local people. My heart does not wish for you to leave at all. I want to go to Doboj with you as your PA.'

'Thank you, Suzanne. Modriča is closer to your house. Why will you be going to Doboj? Doboj is about 60 kilometres from your house. You can't travel on a daily basis, so you should stay here.'

'Yes, I want to be with you,' Suzanne said clearly this time. 'In my mental state, I can no longer live in Prada. I will have no problem leaving Zainab and Suleiman. But it is impossible for me to leave you. Here, we could meet whenever I wanted. But now it seems you are going too far, as if you are going back to your country.'

'I have to go back to India one day. Moreover, the mission rules forbid the intimacy of monitors with their LAs, you know!'

'Ugh, no one obeys those rules. Many LAs have moved to foreign countries with their boyfriends. They have made a rule, but it is not acceptable. Everyone in the mission knows that no one has the right to interfere in individuals' lives. Ignore the rules of the mission,' she said dismissively.

'But you know how strictly I follow the mission rules,' I said the words quite firmly.

'Okay, I'll rent a separate room. I'll see you every day, but I'm coming to Doboj. It's much more tempting for me to have your company than my small savings,' Suzanne's voice was determined as she stared at me with her wide eyes full of tears.

'I will apply to the MHQ for my transfer to Doboj,' Suzanne ran out of my chamber.

On Saturday morning, Suzanne came to my house in Modriča to have breakfast with me.

I greeted her and said, 'You please sit here. I'm making breakfast for both of us.'

'I don't eat boiled eggs, it seems too tasteless; please make omelette with four eggs for me, along with bun and butter.'

I boiled two eggs for myself and put a saucepan on the hot plate to make an omelette. Suzanne liked tomatoes and cheese in her omelette, but when I opened the fridge, there was no cheese. I cracked four eggs and put them in a bowl and chopped tomatoes, raw chillies and onions. Suzanne left the living room and came to the kitchen to help me make breakfast.

'What are these?' she asked me, pointing to the raw chillies.

'Green chillies; they are very hot,' I looked at her and jokingly asked, 'Would you like to have some?' I looked at her and thought, I'll see how stubborn you are! Once you get a taste of the raw chilli, you will understand why we Indians are so stubborn!

Suzanne eagerly said, 'I will try!'

She took a raw chilli in her hand and said, 'I have never seen this before. From where did you find this vegetable?'

'I brought it from Tuzla's Interrex. Boye took me there.'

Suzanne put the bun bread, butter, eggs and banana on the dining table. After getting everything ready, we sat down at the dining table and had our breakfast. While eating, tears flowed from her eyes. Her eyes and face turned red, and the tip of her nose turned brick red. She said to me with a smile on her face, 'It's really very hot, you know?' After a while, she ran to the washroom. I heard the sound of retching from outside.

'Should I come in for any help?'

'No, please don't come, I'll be back soon.'

After a while, Suzanne came out of the washroom. I was scared to see her devastated condition. I took her in my arms and brought her to the bedroom, laid her on the bed, then took off her shoes and put them on the floor.

'You've done this to avoid me, haven't you?' Suzanne asked calmly.

'No, I didn't realize that you would not be able to tolerate it!' I came back to the bedroom with a raw chilli and then started eating it to show Suzanne that chilli wasn't that bad. To reassure Suzanne, I finished the whole chilli in front of her.

Suzanne smiled, 'I know that you won't feed me anything poisonous; I'm 100 per cent sure, but why did you bother to eat it? Do you always eat this vegetable?'

'We regularly eat this in India,' I informed her casually.

After a while, I stared getting hiccups, and I ran to the washroom and threw up. I should not have eaten a whole raw chilli in a bid to be chivalrous! I washed my face and came back to the bedroom. Suzanne grabbed my hand and pulled me to bed, moved closer to embrace me and snuggled her face in my neck.

'Does Srietlana come to you?' Suzanne asked me, whispering very close to my ear.

'No, why? Is she supposed to come to me? Did she say anything?' I asked her in surprise.

'Oh no, I was asking if she comes in your dream. Why are you so excited? In fact, last night, I dreamed that Srietlana was going somewhere far away with you, into a deep forest.'

'Yeah, why should I go with Srietlana?'

'No, I know you won't go with her because you will go with me!' She moved closer and hugged me tightly. Her warm breath under the blanket was making me excited. My body was numb. Was I slowly losing control of myself? Her pink lips seemed to be the most delicious aphrodisiacs in the world. Slowly, very slowly, Suzanne took control of my body. I felt like I was going to explode. The next thing I remember was waking up to the scent of jui (alstonia scholaris) flowers.

Nineteen

It was noon when I reached Doboj, even though it was just 40 kilometres away from Modriča. I met Tariq in the chamber of the regional commander, where he had come to say goodbye to the commander. When he heard that I had come to look for a rented house, he asked me to check his residence out. 'My flat is on the west side of the front park, you can walk to the office, I used to do that in summer. A widow owns the flat. The rent is moderate, and the woman comes and cleans the flat by herself twice a week. The important thing is that Mamma has no other income except this,' Tariq said. 'Sometimes I wonder how she would have survived if she didn't have this apartment to rent out.'

'Okay, let's go see the house and talk to her.'

I went with Tariq to his office, 'This is where you'll be from Monday. I have already sorted my work, but is it okay if I explain it to you when you get here?'

About an hour later, we went down to the parking lot, when we saw Suzanne approaching the car.

When I tried to introduce Tariq to Suzanne, she said, 'I know Tariq, he is from Lahore.'

Tariq smiled, 'Thank you, Suzanne,' and extended his hand towards her.

Suzanne got into my car and we drove back, leaving the regional office on the north of Narodani Heroza Park and Tariq's house on the west. In two minutes, we reached Harizma Apartment, a medium-sized ten-storey house with a neat two-room flat on the third floor. As soon as we got inside Tariq's apartment, which I liked at the very first glance, he called Mamma and informed her about our arrival.

'You will pay the same rent, I'm telling Mamma.'

The landlady arrived promptly, 'My name is Nada Tuloski.' She was a tall Serbian woman, not as timid as the typical Serbian woman as it seemed to me, but her drooping face indicated that old age had taken a heavy toll on her health.

Tariq said, 'You can't find a kinder woman.' As he spoke in Urdu, she couldn't understand. Tariq smiled and said in the local language, 'He will pay whatever I used to pay for the rent, 300 DM.'

'I'll be here by ten o'clock on Monday,' I informed her.

'Tariq leaves tomorrow, I will clean the apartment as soon as he leaves,' she handed me her duplicate key and said, 'Come back whenever you want.'

Tariq pulled out a visiting card from his own country and handed it to me as he said, 'I will probably not see you again anytime soon. Your Hindustan government will not give me visa, and you may not want to come to Pakistan, but I promise, if you ever come to Lahore, I will make all the arrangements for you.'

Suzanne and I bid Tariq goodbye and came out of the apartment, got in the car and drove off to Modriča.

'Great flat, two rooms side by side. I can enjoy the beauty of the park as soon as I open the window. It would be great to be here together! I would go to Prada every Saturday evening, spend some time with my stepmother and brother till Sunday afternoon and then come back to Doboj. There are graves of my father and mother in the field next to the church, and I routinely go there every Sunday. I have already talked to both of them about you.' There was a tone of happiness in her voice, so I kept looking at her with a smile.

She kept on talking as we drove, and at one point, I told her to sing a song for me.

'I'm Real,
Cause I'm Real,
The Way You Walk,
The Way You Move,
The Way You Talk...'

Suzanne sang waving around both her hands, shaking her waist, mimicking Jennifer Lopez. At that moment, Suzanne seemed to be the happiest person on earth.

Daylight was fading away, evenings here were quite different from Calcutta. Even after the sun fully disappeared from the horizon, there remained a faint trail of light in the sky. Most evenings, I couldn't see the bright orange sun at dusk, which almost made me miss our typical sunset. Somehow it made me feel lucky, being born in India. I often wondered how the stories from my childhood, the stories of Bangama-Bangami, Shankchunni or Mechho Petni would have been written if they originated in this country, under a different-looking sun.

'These evenings must bring up a lot of nostalgic memories for you. Wait till summer, it's wonderful, and this gloominess you complain of will go away,' Suzanne assured me.

When we got back to the Modriča station around half past seven, Suzanne got off at the parking lot, and walked to her car, 'See you tomorrow at noon, bye.'

I met Liam as he was coming out of the station. We exchanged hugs, and he asked, 'Have you found a home yet?'

'Yeah, I did. Thanks for asking. I've some pending work here now, after completing those, I'll leave Modriča tomorrow. We may not meet again after that.'

'Hey, no, we may meet again sure, we are on the same mission!' Liam left with a big smile.

I went to my chamber and wrote a note for my successor so that he would not have any difficulty in understanding the role after I was gone.

Arriving at the station post-lunch on Sunday, I found it almost desolate. Once I was satisfied with the reports, I emailed them to the MHQ. I was about to get up and leave when Suzanne came and stood beside me.

'When did you come?' I looked into her eyes and asked.

'About half an hour ago.' She handed me a piece of paper and said, 'Recommend this application. I have already mailed a soft copy, but I'll send a hard copy too.'

I checked the application and signed it.

Suzanne mailed the application to the MHQ, stating that she wanted to work with me in Doboj. As I was working closely with the people of Bosnia and because I'd positively influenced a lot in Suzanne's activities on the mission, she wanted to work with me for a little longer, in Human Rights.

'Is it not a little exaggerated? The MHQ may take this as a fishy affair!' I said.

'Oh no, it's fine, leave it to me. I've seen it happen many times. The LAs are tagged with the monitors in the same way they tag the UN car,' Suzanne appeared confident.

'Wait, please tell me the password for your email. I'll also send a letter with strong recommendation from your email so they don't reject my application.' Pulling up a chair next to me, she leaned over and emailed from my address to the chief of the personnel section, which read, 'I am very comfortable working with Suzanne Grabovich as my language assistant. She is very competent, and if possible, I would like her to continue as my language assistant in Doboj as well.' Suzanne moved even closer and I felt her breasts against my body, I was mesmerized by her scent, and my brain was not working, I forgot how to react.

'It's getting a bit childish, don't you think! They won't accept this, it'll just make everyone laugh,' I told Suzanne.

'There is nothing childish about it, so many people have

done it before and got what they wanted. Mission just bothers about the work, and they don't care much about private matters of their personnel,' Suzanne said with great confidence. 'Go home, you won't find anyone at the station anymore.'

After shutting the computer down, I said goodbye to my first posting and left. Suzanne followed me to my house in her car and helped me pack my luggage. She herself called the landlord to clear the house rent, took a receipt from him and put it in my suitcase.

Suzanne looked at me with wide eyes and said, 'I want to stay the night here. My heart doesn't want to leave you alone right now. There are very few people in the world who love me, so when I look at you, I feel like a helpless puppy.'

'It will seem very odd, particularly when it is the last night here. Please go back home, we are going to meet in a day or two anyways,' I replied.

She became sentimental and hugged me several times. The two of us walked down the street. I walked her to her car, and before she got in, she kissed me on my cheek and on my lips, and finally said goodbye. 'Don't worry, I will come by Tuesday or Wednesday,' she said.

I stared at the tail light of Suzanne's car for a while until the red light faded into the distant street. Was that my heart palpitating? I put my hand on my chest to try to understand the feeling.

I dragged my exhausted body up the stairs to my apartment on the second floor. My mind was heavy, I didn't know why I was worrying that I might now work with Suzanne again but my journey with her was destined to end there. Suzanne may not be posted in Doboj! This thought was consuming me from within, and a strange restlessness overpowered me completely. I came down to the street again like a ghost chasing a teenager.

I went to the spot on the road where Suzanne had stood

just a while ago. Somehow, I felt that this was our last meeting. With an unhinged mind, I started walking aimlessly, with snow under my feet. A dim soft colourless light shrouded the world around me, as the night remained silent, still. I found myself under a leafless apple tree, with snow on my face. I looked up at the sky; a half-eaten moon was faintly visible, leaning against a cosmic darkness far away in the distance. I was trembling like an adolescent fool in the wide extent of the lonely world, with the moon as my only friend. Was it for the clouds that I couldn't see the moon clearly? I wondered. Or maybe she was going somewhere, maybe she was searching for her lover too, wandering across the black emptiness of the night sky, all alone. I looked at the moon and I started following her. I had to know if she would find her lover.

I didn't realize how far I had come when then moon disappeared and brought me back to reality. Standing at a crossroads, I was trembling in fear and cold as I felt my heart beating loudly. Looking around, trying desperately to make sense of where I was, I noticed the tall wireless tower at the Modriča IPTF station.

I walked towards the tower and came back to my house. I was worried if Suzanne had reached home safely. I ran up to the second floor, picked up the car key from the table and ran downstairs, and drove off. It was as though I could still see the red tail light of Suzanne's car trailing off in front of me.

Eventually, I reached Prada to find Suzanne's car parked in front of their house. Suzanne came down running as I was turning my car around. She must have heard the engine.

As Suzanne approached, I was compelled to stop the car and got out. She reached out and hugged me, 'United Nations Unite, We Are United, We Are United Nations!' The famous UN slogan became intertwined in Suzanne's inflated voice.

'I was walking and looking at the moon and I lost it. I was

worried about not seeing you again.' I whispered to Suzanne.

She smiled, kissed me and said, 'The moon is still there, silly, you just couldn't see it!'

In her white thin veil-like nightgown, she looked like a bouquet of jasmine.

She moved the curtains away from her window as we got to her room, and with an enticing smile, she said, 'Look, you can see the moon again.'

Suzanne went ahead and cranked up the heater of the room. She pushed me gently on the bed, took all my clothes off one by one and wrapped me up completely with her warm supple embrace. I could clearly see the half-moon still floating in the night sky, with a bright radiant glow.

I woke up at eight in the morning alongside a tall bouquet of jasmine flowers beside me on the bed. Suzanne was still sleeping. I touched her cheeks as she laid there with a visage of absolute contentment.

Without waking her up, I quietly used the bathroom, got dressed and went downstairs, where I met Zainab on the ground floor. She asked me to join her for breakfast.

'I'm sorry, I'm kind of in a hurry, and I'll come again soon.' I got into my car and drove off.

I came back home, had breakfast and left with two huge suitcases full of my stuff. The house owner came to bid me goodbye. I thanked him and smiled.

Bye, Modriča! Goodbye, Suzanne!

I drove off on the road to Doboj, leaving behind Dragomir's house.

Familiar houses, familiar shops, familiar roads were slowly disappearing. I did not know if I would ever come back to Modriča again in my life. The sadness of leaving Modriča behind was palpable as I looked outside with tears in my eyes.

Twenty

After reaching Doboj, I went straight to Harijma's apartment. I opened the door with the key given by the landlady, unpacked my luggage and took a quick bath before I got ready and went out to the new office.

When I joined work, Regional Commander Maria Grazdanova came to talk to me. This forty-eight-year-old sweet lady said that she was from Ukraine and it was her third UN mission. She had previously worked in Croatia for two years, in Brčko for one year, before she came here about three months ago. Suddenly, she asked, 'Will you come with me to Sarajevo? I have a half-hour meeting at the MHQ. Then I'll take you around the SFOR canteens of the US and Denmark, see if you like those.'

I thought it would not be wise to refuse the request of the Regional Commander on the very first day, so I agreed to go to Sarajevo. I called my LA, Dragana Petrovich, and said, 'I'm going to Sarajevo with Maria. Please attend the office and keep the translated copies ready on my table, in case there's any important correspondence.'

Maria said, 'You don't have to take the car, we'll go and come back together.' So, I became Maria's companion on the road for about 170 kilometres. From our initial encounter, I assumed she was a very fragile, soft-spoken and slow-moving woman, but I was mistaken.

She hit the gears like a pro and kicked off the car at a great speed. Although there was no snow or heavy traffic on the road, I did not expect such a calm woman to drive so fast.

She continued chattering about all sorts of things as we flew by every signpost on the road. She had a twenty-three-year-old son and a twenty-one-year-old daughter at home. Maria said that there was a marked resemblance between her son and me, which made her want to see them. I thought to myself that all human beings had this same emotion, no matter how different or which corner of the world they came from, it was only human.'

It was nice to be in Sarajevo. After Maria left for the meeting, I went to the second floor to use the internet. I checked my emails first, then I started reading the Bengali newspapers of Calcutta. Despite being in a place like Bosnia, amongst all the terror and violence around me, I could feel my heart beating faster from reading the news. My mind was overrun with all kinds of questions:

Have we truly entered the twenty-first century?

Is India really a secular, democratic country?

Do we not see people here in the guise of God too?

Maria kept her word, as she came back in about an hour. She stood in front of me, smiled and said, 'I have finished my work, I can now take you on a tour the city.'

As Maria was getting into the car, she said, 'The SRSG (Special Representative of the Secretary-General of the UN), Mr Jacques Paul Klein, had a meeting with all the units. On behalf of the IPTF, there was the Commissioner, Regional Commanders, CJAU (Criminal Justice Advisory Unit), CAU (Civil Affairs Unit), Chief of Human Rights, PAO (Public Affairs Unit). The SRSG was happy with the work of the United Nations in Bosnia; the progress has been more than expected. He'll report accordingly to Secretary General Kofi Annan. It has been possible because of the impartial attitude and hard work of good officers like you.'

'Thank you, but, in fact, all the officers I've met here are very experienced and efficient,' I argued.

'Your country has sent the best unit of officers for these missions, I have to admit. I have seen the officers sent by the European and Latin American countries too, and to be frank, their performance has been objectively less impressive. That is also why there is no special set of tasks assigned to them. The success of the work we're doing depends on a few hard-working officers like you.'

'You know, Maria, here is an interesting observation of mine. Apparently, we are able to work for a cause in the international community, being as neutral as one can possibly be. But when it comes to matters of our own country, somehow, we are always inclined towards one political party or the other, and we end up losing our impartiality.'

As the conversation went on, it became clear to me that Maria, too, had the fair ability to do her own analysis.

We walked around looking at the NATO-bombed Press Club building, where the Serbian army was stationed during the war. There were three hundred and fifty year-old Ottoman Turk mosques, as well as an Orthodox Church and a Catholic Church. Maria said, 'Sarajevo is called the Jerusalem of the Balkans because of its mosques and churches.'

Then we took the Downtown Road, and Maria showed me the infamous spot where Archduke Franz Ferdinand of Austria and his wife Sophie were shot dead by Dragutin Dimitrijević, the head of the Serbian Military Intelligence. The assassination took place on 28 June 1914, on the Latin Bridge over the Miljacka River. In addition to Gavrilo Princip, five other people were directly involved in the horrific assassination.

Archduke Ferdinand had arrived in Sarajevo by train from the Ilidza Spa that morning to visit the Sarajevo Military Barracks, where he was met by the police chief and the mayor of the city. According to the prior arrangement, Archduke Ferdinand, his wife Sophie, Governor Oskar Potiorek and a lieutenant colonel were supposed to address the audience after the inspection. Accidentally, he boarded the third motor car which was open-hooded, in the six-car motorcade from Sarajevo station. Meanwhile, the six-member team of assailants took their positions on the road, waiting with bombs and pistols.

'Here, the assailants hid in disguise for their targets; they all had Belgian FN 1910 pistols and bombs in their hands,' Maria said after crossing the Latin Bridge, stopping her car on one particular spot on the side of the road.

I got out of the car, took a deep breath and looked to the right at the riverbank, where there were rows of food shops. For a moment, I was transported to that fateful day, watching the events unfold before my eyes.

The day it happened, it was at around ten o'clock in the morning when the Archduke's convoy crossed the bridge to visit the military barracks. Positioned on that spot by the road, two assassins were waiting for their target, but as it would happen, they could not find a suitable spot for a clear shot. Desperately, the third assassin, Nedeljko Čabrinović, dropped a bomb on Ferdinand's car. Luckily, the bomb missed the Archduke, as it was dropped on the hood of the car and ended up exploding under the fourth vehicle of the convoy. About twenty people were seriously injured. The assassin immediately chewed on a cyanide capsule that was hanging from his neck, but he was unsuccessful in his attempt to take his own life as the fatal effect of that cyanide capsule he consumed had expired. Those who came to see the Archduke, chased Čabrinović before he jumped into the Miljacka River to escape the mob. But as fate would have it, the river was almost dried up in the summer, and he was promptly caught in the knee-deep water by the angry crowd. Police arrived soon after and rescued him from being lynched by the mob. Princip stood there and watched the whole episode, his jaws tightened as he patiently waited on for

Archduke's return journey to take another chance.

Archduke Ferdinand was furious after the episode and expressed his absolute dissent in his speech in the town hall. 'Mr Mayor, a royal delegate has been invited to come and give a speech and he will be bombarded? What does this say about your administration and law and order system?' he exclaimed. Everyone was unresponsive.

Before the scheduled visit of the Archduke, the Police Chief had recommended several times that the security be tightened by bringing in extra force, but the repeated warnings were ignored. Later that day, the Governor General tried to manage the stage show by rallying the motorcade through the city. Without being properly briefed, the driver took the apple cove on the bank of the Miljaka River and reached the Latin Bridge. As the convoy was about to take a wrong turn, the Governor shouted and the startled driver pressed the brake all of a sudden. And the long-awaited opportunity had finally arrived for Princip. Without wasting a single moment, he climbed on to the footboard of the car and from his pistol, fired a shot that hit the Archduke on his neck. The assassin then fired another shot at his wife, Sophie. She fell to the ground. Despite the agony of his fatal wound, the Archduke cried out, 'Sophie, please don't die.' They were rushed to the Governor's house, and later both succumbed to their injuries.

Right after shooting the Archduke and his family, Princip tried to take his own life by shooting himself, but as he was quickly surrounded by police and the mob, his plan to escape arrest and trial failed just like his comrade.

Anti-Serb movements spread throughout the city of Sarajevo. The movement gradually spread to the whole of Croatia, including Bosnia of the Austro-Hungarian Empire. Bosnian Governor Oskar Potiorek instigated the movement. Many Serbs' homes, shops and businesses were burnt, and some Serbs died in the fire of public grievance.

The flare of revenge gradually spread out across Europe as the incipient disturbances gradually grew, and it was no longer possible to suppress the outbursts, which eventually set the stage for the beginning of World War I.

Maria and I were moving around the city of Sarajevo, and I stopped in front of a multistoreyed house. Seeing me stare at the bullet marks on the building, Maria asked, 'Haven't you seen such signs of bullet rain before?'

'No, we didn't have much time to go around during our initial training. I used to come to the MHQ building at ten in the morning and return at half past six in the evening after finishing my training. As soon as we finished training, we were posted at different stations. So, I have not seen these remnants of war before.'

'These buildings are a testimony to the extent of Serbian Army machine gun fire. You will find such bullet marks in many houses in the village too. Not just these, the skeletons of houses blown up with grenades or rockets are not uncommon either.' There was a hint of remorse in Maria's voice.

As evening descended, we reached the city centre, where we ate *ćepavi* (much like sheek kebab) and bread at Alejia Hotel. We also briefly went shopping in the army canteen to pick up tax-free commodities that are so much cheaper than normal markets.

While she was shopping for herself, Maria gifted me a black leather hat, on the premise that wearing a black hat would make me look smarter. At half past seven, we left for Doboj. This part of the evening we spent having casual conversations, and at one point she mentioned how much she was missing her son and daughter.

Then, we stopped in Zenica, and Maria bought two cans of Coke for us. After the drink, we drove off again when she asked, 'Do you have any difficulty working at UNMIBH?'

I shook my head and said, 'No, not at all, I'm quite comfortable here.'

'You know, the work of seven IPTF stations means that you have to supervise the human rights violations reported at thirty-three local police stations?'

I nodded and said, 'Dragana gave me the list of police stations before we left today. I asked her to make a list of how many petitions and enquiries were pending in these stations.'

'Well, get to work, I have told the IPTF Commissioner about you today. He is very happy with your working style, this time you may get the UN medal.'

∽

The next day, I took up the work that Tariq had left behind. I told Dragana that everything needed to be systematized and asked her to sort everything out, and to show me some of the most important complaints, which I would handle myself. Two days later, in the evening, as I was walking out of my office building, I heard Dragana's voice calling out my name. There was something off in her tone, which surprised me a little at first, but as I turned back, she walked right up to me. The smell of her light perfume reached my nose.

I remembered the perfume I had gifted Suzanne had a similar scent. Since I had arrived here, I noticed this strange similarity among all the LAs, where they all dress up in a somewhat similar fashion, be it the type of clothes, the hairstyles, the shoes or the perfume. I had once asked Suzanne, 'Why do you all have almost the same style?'

'Silly,' she had smiled and said, 'We are all after the trendy clothes we see in Hollywood.'

Sometimes I wondered if I was really that oblivious to the

matters of the opposite gender, or if I understood women at all.

Suzanne had once said to me, 'Compliment women on how they look. Girls always love to hear it.' One day, I had told her that she looked like Saira Banu from Bollywood. When she saw Saira Banu in a film for the first time, I could see the sparkle in her eyes when she said, 'I am just like her, like a copy, only my eyes are a different colour!' Then she asked me if Saira Banu was popular in India.

'Oh, she is, yes. She is quite famous, in fact, very well known as one of the top heroines in the Indian film industry of her time, and men are crazy about her too. That's why I compared you with her.'

I remember she had laughed and said, 'That's one way to compliment, I guess. That's good!' She sighed then and said, 'How come you never say anything about how I dress, wear my hair or make-up, or anything about my clothes or shoes?'

'From now on, I will,' I had replied.

But I never got around to doing that.

Dragana was looking at me with a hint of smile in the corner of her lips. I felt relief in that it wasn't probably any bad news all of a sudden. She handed me a paper, which read: 'After due consideration, Suzanne Grabovic's request for transfer to Doboj Regional Office has been rejected.' I received this copy of their reply because previously I had forwarded a copy of her application to the chief of personnel section.

I imagined Suzanne would have received the news herself by then and I felt sorry for her. I didn't have a mobile phone, otherwise she would have called.

Dragana left promptly right after handing me the paper; she didn't wait to see my reaction. I hope Dragana eventually realized that I didn't have any dissatisfaction with her competence and that my recommendation for Suzanne was merely a preference based on our prolonged association.

Suzanne was alone in the world; she lost her mother in her childhood and her father in her early youth. She had said, 'I would have left this Prada already if my parents' graves, my father's house and his orchard were not here.' Zainab and Suleiman never let her feel that they were not her own family, but still she had tears in her eyes every time she remembered her mother's voice or her father's face.

Sometimes she would say in a feeble voice, 'I am so alone!' When she used to go to her parents' grave on Sundays, Suzanne forcibly kept a smile on her face, but her mind cried a lot just thinking about them. Resting a few feet underneath the ground, the dead lied there still, in eternal peace; they couldn't feel the resonance of the sorrowful tunes of Suzanne's heart. Suzanne would walk up to their graves, talk to her late mom and dad separately all while carrying a smile so that the departed would know how happy she was in her life.

My mind was so occupied with her thoughts that I forgot I had my car parked in the parking lot of the regional office, and walked across the Narodnih Heroja Park and reached my new apartment at Harizma. My mind was in a state of bitter sadness as I entered my room.

I heard a knock on the door and I opened it, and not to my surprise, Suzanne was standing in front of me. She was wearing a white gown, and her face looked extremely pale, as if someone had drained all the blood out of her. She looked at me and smiled. I could see tears in her eyes mingled with laughter. Her smile soaked my mind, and seeing that I was staring at her in silence, she came forward and hugged me. Her body was shaking and I could almost feel her tremble.

She cried for a while, her hands wrapped around me. I hugged her even tighter to comfort and support her, with my hands moving down her head and across her back. She dragged me to the bed and climbed on top of me. Her lips were pressing against mine, I closed my eyes and I felt her warm tongue inside my mouth, which tasted rather strange. I've always noticed the smell of a flower in the scent of her body, this time, however, the smell was similar to that of camphor, as if coming from a grave. Suzanne started undressing; I grabbed her and pulled her close to me as I desperately wanted to feel her skin against mine. I ran my fingers through her golden hair, but it came off in my hand as if it was a wig. I touched her skull, only to realize that the warmth of her skin suddenly disappear, turning her lips stiff, as cold as a rock. With a big jolt, I opened my eyes and saw that I was kissing a skeleton.

My body was soaked in sweat. I got out of the bed and cranked up the central heating system to cool the room down. At midnight, it seemed like winter was slowly fading away from the Bosnian sky in the northern hemisphere. I walked to the toilet in the dark to wash my face in the cold water. But there was a salty taste on my tongue.

Twenty-one

As I arrived at the office the next morning, I got a phone call from Suzanne. Before I could say anything, she informed me that Suleiman had been arrested by the Šamac Police without mentioning any reason for his arrest. She said she was going to the Šamac Police Station, worried about what was to come.

I was really surprised hearing about Suleiman being arrested. I liked that man. In his demeanour, I had never noticed anything that gave me a reason to suspect him of any wrongdoings. He was studying engineering, and I had seen a picture of him with a guitar on a wall in Zainab's room. He used to sing 'people's songs', as I liked to call them. I had once told him, 'I would love to listen to you someday, singing for your people.'

Suzane hung up the phone after I wished her luck. It struck to me that Šamac Police Station was, in fact, within my zone, but the IPTF never usually bother with local issues, although they might enquire if something went wrong. If that was the case, I could find out the details myself, and Suzanne probably knew this. I thought to myself: is that why she called me, to find out what was going on?

All these thoughts were going through my mind when Dragana knocked on the door. She entered my office with a bunch of papers in her hand, sat on the chair in front and calmly said, 'These are for you. When you go through them, if you have any difficulty in understanding, could you come to my table, please? Actually, the doctor advised me not to stand or do repetitive physical movements, because of my pregnancy.'

'That's great news! Congratulations!' I said with a smile,

'Please do take care of yourself. It's alright, I'll come to you if I need anything.'

Ignoring my congratulatory message and after some small talk, she stared aimlessly at me and went on to talking about her personal matters, 'I want to have this child. You see, I am struggling a lot with this decision too as I am still alone. But the thing is, I still want to be a mother. My boyfriend and my parents are against my decision. They say I'm twenty-four, so it's not the right age for this, it's the time to enjoy life. What I find hard to understand is that if motherhood gives me enjoyment, why can't others accept that instead of interfering with my private life?'

Dragana said that although her mother was sympathetic to her, she couldn't go beyond her father's final words of approval. Even in a war-ridden place, on this side of the world, I found the woman's voice being outweighed by that of her husband. Was I in Doboj or Dubrajpur?

I said, 'It's strange. I assumed people had a different attitude towards these situations in developed countries such as yours.'

'Do you think the men here are any different than in your country? Men always want to dominate everything, wishing to force their opinions on others, especially women. I could enjoy the ecstasy of sex—that is fine. But as seen by men, if I have a child of my own, I would suddenly be defying the responsibility of pleasing them. What kind of mentality is it, do you think?' she responded fiercely.

'Only your opinions should matter in the end because the baby is in your womb,' I said.

She slapped the table loudly with both hands and exclaimed, 'Yes! You are right, the baby is in my womb and it's now an integral part of my body. Why can't others understand this simple fact?'

I told her with a sigh, 'Look, everything will be alright,

eventually. Let the baby come first!'

Dragana was a very hard-working girl and quite efficient. She could produce the records of all thirty-three police stations and seven IPTF stations in no time, and I was really impressed. I asked her, 'You're quite good, how do you do this so fast and so efficiently?'

She didn't seem to take heed of my compliments and laughed, 'I keep these notes on my computer according to my personal system. I update them little by little every day so I can track everything and let anyone know any time about any update.'

A few days later, Siddhartha was also transferred from Zenica to Doboj. I told him to stay with me in my apartment, but he politely declined. His wife and daughter were scheduled to visit him next summer, so he decided to rent a house a kilometre away. However, he spent most of his time with me. During the day, we used to go home and cook as per our shifts, but we cooked together at night in one place. Then, we would have dinner together and spend some time before Siddhartha would drive to his place.

Siddhartha joined the SRU (Special Response Unit) team at the Doboj Regional Office. The task of the SRU team was to find loopholes in the old laws of Bosnia-Herzegovina, to make proposals for legislation in the form of democratic laws, to send them to the government, and to interpose the laws into the laws of post-war countries under the supervision of the UN. The pressure from the UN to bring equality among the people of this nation was almost tangible.

I introduced Siddhartha to Maria one day, 'We are both from the same city—Calcutta. We are also officers from the same batch.'

The three of us had got together for coffee in the canteen. Maria said 'Well, normally this rarely happens. You rarely get to spend time with your own people. But I have a request, you should treat me to that mutton curry of yours one day. In a mission in Pakistan, I once had that delicacy, and it was fantastic to say the least.'

∽

Even though my shift ended at five o'clock, I could never leave on time, and it would almost always be half past five or even six when I would finally leave office.

It had been over a week without a trace of Suzanne when she called me panting over the phone, 'You are not always available in the office! Why don't you buy a cell phone?'

'Yeah, either I'm busy in a meeting or with an enquiry, but usually I remain in the office in the first half. I wanted to keep my mental peace intact without having a mobile. However, now I am finally thinking of getting one,' I told her.

'I am working with Liam now, so, here's the thing, my brother was caught in a sedation case. Police alleged that my brother wanted to start a revolution on Bosnian soil again by writing songs and singing. But you know that he is not a revolutionary at all.' Suzanne paused and said, 'Does talking about common people, their misery, pain and sufferings mean revolution? Don't people have the right to talk about finding the missing persons? If the government doesn't disagree with the independent ideas, is it tantamount to treason?'

'Why aren't you complaining before the judiciary?'

'Yeah, that sounds pretty far-fetched to me. I have to bring Suleiman out of jail first. If we go to protest against the police now, they might throw him in the tribunal to start a trial, and he would be stuck there much longer. I am following the advice of my lawyer. I'll come to you after sorting these things out, and I will do my office work from there.'

At the beginning of April, the usual haziness in the atmosphere started to taper off, and from the Bosnian town to the village market, everything glittered under the golden sunlight. The snow completely disappeared from the roads, the trees and even from the hills far away. Most of the trees stood with leafless stumps, resembling an age-old decayed mummy.

One day, I woke up early, and as I pulled aside the heavy curtains from the window, the soft golden light of the morning sun shimmering in the distant horizon flooded my entire room. I could not remember when was the last time I saw such a magnificent sunrise. Meanwhile, as the winter season was drawing to an end, the days started to get progressively longer. The sun went down almost at half past seven. Returning from the office, I would go out with Siddhartha to the beautiful small hills of Usora, Teslić, Zavidovići and Maglaj. We discovered many more villages, while we drove around, listening to Rabindra Sangeet, Hemanta-Sandhya and Rafi-Lata-Kishore, exploring something new every day. On the way back, I sometimes used to go to the small village of Yella, near Doboj, to procure fresh vegetables and spices from Fatima, who would laugh every time I said '*Dobre Viche* (Good evening)'. I would often come back to the flat with some kind of meat, like *domac* (native chicken) or maybe *janjetina* (lamb). Siddhartha loved to cook as well, and we would often take turns preparing different dishes.

Towards the end of April, the flowers started to blossom, which were pure white at first, with a hint of pink, and then slowly turned yellow, followed by an explosion of colours in a sea of thousands of flowers. Those trees were still devoid of any leaves and there would be flowers everywhere. Wherever I looked, different colours—maroon, red, blue and yellow—entirely covered the vast grounds like a soft blanket.

I didn't have to wear a jacket anymore. The leaves on the trees started to appear slowly, then they gradually became golden green. By the end of first week of May, my sweater lost all its use.

As May came to an end, local markets became flooded with a variety of vegetables, such as cauliflower, cabbage, tomatoes, eggplant, capsicum, watermelon, cucumber and many more. I was surprised to see the sheer size of the pumpkins and gourds.

'Let's go to Tuzla, I've heard a lot about the lakes there,' Siddhartha said one day, 'Invite your LA Saira Banu, too, for this tour, have fun, enjoy the city and let the gentle spring breeze blow both of you away. The stories of your hearts will echo in the romantic evenings of the lakeside cafes…'

I had to stop Siddhartha, 'You are becoming a poet day by day. When's your family coming here?'

'They will arrive in about twenty days.'

'Okay, but Suzanne will not be able to come. Her brother has been arrested by the police in a sedation case and taken away to Sarajevo. Our regional office instructed us not to interfere in this case, as someone from the MHQ is monitoring the matter.'

'Does that mean that UN put veto on your work?'

'Yep. That is what it is apparently. My mind is saying that Suleiman is going to face a lot of trouble. Leave it be, we'll see if we can bring someone else.'

Siddhartha thought for a moment and said, 'We can take Tatiana Mihailovic from our team. In fact, I often hear a lot about Tuzla from her. Let's go next Sunday morning.'

'Sure. Let's do that.'

As per our plan, Siddhartha came to my house at eight on Sunday. By then, I was already dressed. We drove to the back of the housing complex behind the park, picked up Tatiana and promptly started our journey.

Tatiana shook my hand and said, 'I'm Tatiana, but you can call me Tania, that's what I'm called at home.'

Siddhartha drove out of town. Leaving the Modriča-Sarajevo Road behind, we crossed the Bosna River, when Tatiana said,

'We'll go through Graçanicë, the distance is about 65 kilometres and the road is decent.' We were driving along the ridge of the hill, with a beautiful view of greenery by the road.

'Tuzla is the largest city in the north-east of Bosnia. Coal, ignite, rock salt and other minerals are extracted from here. All these hillocks you are seeing, these are all extensions of the Majevica mountain range,' she informed us.

The road was serpentine, with a few dried-up streams flowing over the road, the tide of flowers and green leaves on the hill, faint fountains with scanty water running down the asphalt road. Tatiana said, 'As soon as the rains start, these streams will rejuvenate, even though they might appear to be struggling to keep their existence now.'

After a quarter of an hour's drive, we reached the town of Tuzla. Raising her hand, pointing towards what looked like a dried-up canal, Tatiana said, 'It's a river.' She shook her head and said, 'I know you don't believe it to be a river. In the coming rainy season, you would definitely believe that!'

'I will surely come, it is impossible to see everything in one day!' Siddhartha said.

Twenty-two

Tatiana was our guide for the day, 'The Ottoman Turks, due to the abundance of rock salt, called this place Sally. Until ten million years ago, the Pannonian Sea existed here. Now, it has dried up and turned into a lake. In the Tuzla town, there are three lakes—one big and two small ones.'

Siddhartha said, 'Being a history student, I know about Eastern European history. However, there is nothing mentioned about small places like Tuzla in the books.'

'I am a student of English literature. But from my limited knowledge of Tuzla, I know that the region was under the rule of different regimes over the years. After four hundred years of rule, the Ottoman Turks fell. Tuzla came under the Sanjak of Javornik and later joined the Austro-Hungarian Empire in the late nineteenth century. After World War I, Tuzla was occupied by the Yugoslavia-Croatia partnership. After World War II, it came under the leadership of Marshal Tito's forces. Bosnia-Herzegovina declared independence in the early nineties of the twentieth century along with the Yugoslav National Army invading and occupying Tuzla. Before the Srebrenica Massacre, in May 1995, the Tuzla Massacre occurred, wherein the Yugoslavian army hacked to death 71 Bosniaks,' Tatiana said. We entered Tuzla by crossing the hill roads and a bridge over the Jala River. Tatiana said, 'Since people are offering their morning prayer, or namaz, now, we will start with the Atiq Mosque, built by Behram Beg 130 years ago.'

When we entered the mosque premises, I had goosebumps. The three of us took off our shoes and stepped into the mosque.

The magical pink over white interior of the mosque had a light-blue coating. Tatiana then led us to the Slobode Square, where we found a fountain in the middle of all the beautiful pink buildings. 'There are only a few people here this morning, but in the evening, a lot of people gather here, chatting, singing, talking and relaxing. It can be called the heart of the city.'

We then went to a cafeteria called Mesut's and ordered burek and melajko coffee (coffee with milk). Finding a local woman with two foreign customers, the owner of the cafeteria, named Mehmedullah, came up to interact with us as we sat down with our coffee. But when Siddhartha raised the issue of the Bosnian conflict, he became completely silent, got up and left the place on the pretext of making coffee.

Tatiana said, 'Everyone here wants to forget about the war. The memory is still fresh, so we all avoid the discussion about the war. We all suffered in one way or another in the four years the civil war lasted. Most of the army men, from the commander to the common soldier, are either in jail or absconding. They are either hiding in some unknown village like a wild animal, for fear of getting caught and going to jail any day. They are living a nightmare. But the blood on their hands will not go away, we all know that, right?' Tatiana's ponytail swayed like a snake's hood every time she shook her head.

Siddhartha said, 'I agree with you, but I still want to have a dossier of all the facts. We have come here from so far. It will also find mention in history books for people to learn.'

'Huh, people will learn? Even in this twenty-first century, people can be incited in the name of religion. Even today, people can commit any atrocity at any moment. Are you happy that people were burnt alive in Ahmedabad or some other places a few months ago? Are these people involved in peace? Have you ever asked the hero whether he is at peace when he cut out a foetus from his mother's womb with a sword? After so much that had already happened, someone else has been benefitting out of such violence! Is this what it takes to ascend to a throne that is soaked in another's blood?' I looked at Tatiana's face redden with rage. She said, 'Sorry, we've all been affected by this civil war, so we get emotional when we discuss it. Let's go to the Garadakač Castle. It was conquered by Captain Hussain Gradasevich, an Ottoman Turk.'

We got in the car and reached Garadakač Castle in ten minutes. However, the fort was closed, so we turned around and sat on the grass. 'The construction of this fort was completed in 1821. The fort was built by the Romans, but the Ottoman Turks captured it in 1831. The walls of this 18-metre-high fort made of large stones are very thick and strong, with a 22-metre-high watchtower,' said Tatiana.

An elderly caretaker was sitting alone on a bench near the gate. A gust of cold air blew over my head. While observing the caretaker sitting relaxed, the fort came into life in front of my eyes. The noise was deafening. I clearly saw two very alert sentries standing like statues on either side of the gate, with long bayonet guns in their hands.

I lost track of time. Siddhartha tapped me on the head and said, 'Where were you lost, my friend?' Siddhartha's voice brought me out of my reverie.

Tatiana said, 'Now let's go to Pannonian Lake.'

Reaching the lake, we parked our car under a tree and walked to the lake.

Tatiana said, 'It is more crowded on this side. Let's go on the other side.'

Walking along the shore of the lake, I saw many young men and women on the street, under the trees, kissing. The expression of love on Bosnian soil was quite clear. Following my gaze, Tatiana said, 'Don't ask me if there is any history behind this kissing scene. Traditionally, I have seen that the aspiration of men and women to kiss is more in Tuzla and this desire is more aroused when the visitors come to the edge of the swimming pool.'

Many men and women dressed in colourful clothes were floating like ducks in the water of the lake, while others were relaxing on the roadside or on the benches of the park.

'Sahib-memsahib's open sunbathing is a beautiful sight, what do you say?' Siddhartha said, walking beside me.

I had heard about the beauty of Balkan women, but if I had not come to this lake in summer, maybe the actual meaning of Balkan beauty would have eluded me. As soon as we crossed the swimming area, we saw pubs in rows and some small restaurants towards the back. It was yet to be lunchtime, so I crossed the pubs and saw an area surrounded by a long rope along the water of the lake.

Tatiana said, 'Water is deeper in this side and this is the boating zone; if you want, you can go for boating before your lunch.'

Siddhartha and I looked at Tatiana. Siddhartha asked, 'You are also coming with us, aren't you?'

Tatiana clarified this time, 'I shall take your leave for some time.'

'I mean, where are you going? Where will you have lunch?'

'I will go to an acquaintance's house a kilometre away; I'll eat something there and come back to join you post-lunch.'

I said, 'Come on, we will drop you.'

'Thank you very much, but I will manage. I'll get back by three o'clock.'

Siddhartha and I looked at each other, then walked towards the boats waiting in the jetty.

Siddhartha said, 'Let's go for boating. In the presence of the lady, there was no advantage of bargaining.'

I shook my head and said, 'Yes, in presence of girls, we

obviously feel ashamed to bargain in a miserly way!'

We reduced the price by half to the boatman's declared rate and got on to the boat. The boatman started the engine and headed towards deep water.

I looked at Siddhartha and said, 'The son of the soil from Kankurgachhi is floating around in Pannonia Lake by boat! What a paradox!'

'From where are you coming, my boy? As far as I know, you have come from a godforsaken remote village of Medinipur district, isn't it?'

The water had no salty taste, though Tatiana said that its water was saline. This time, Siddhartha took a handful of the water and put it in his mouth.

'No, no, it is slightly saline; try it once again.' I saw some people were fishing very attentively.

From the boat we had an expansive view of the flowering trees planted on the shore and the restaurants on the bank on this huge lake. Once we got off the boat, we had a hearty lunch with *čevapi* and *somun* bread at a restaurant of my choice.

Afterwards, just as we were back at the parking lot, we saw Tatiana approaching us with a smile.

Siddhartha said, 'Sabyasachi, you drive. I want a sound sleep for some time. I did not sleep well at night.'

'You should at least visit Freedom Square and the Kapija Memorial and then go to sleep,' Tatiana requested.

We drove to Freedom Square, surrounded by a few statues and a huge open space with many old buildings, some modern buildings and a few big shops. Tatiana said that the old houses here were replicas of some Austrian houses, same as Europe's other squares, surrounded by coffee shops and restaurants.

We had coffee at Freedom Square and went to Kapija Memorial.

'Please stop the car here and come down for a while. Stand

in front of the memorial once more and pray that an event as such does not happen anywhere else in the world.'

Following Tatiana's request, we got out of the car and stood in front of the white marble memorial plaque for a few minutes. From the side, Tatiana said, 'It was nine o'clock in the evening on 25 May 1995 when teenagers and young people had gathered here to celebrate the birthday of Marshal Tito. Suddenly, from a small distant hill, Mount Ozren, Serbian troops dropped mortar shells that killed 71people and grievously injured 250 others.

Tatiana took out a small bouquet of flowers from her shoulder bag, knelt down in front of the memorial plaque and placed the bouquet in front of it with tears in her eyes. She remained seated in the same position for about two minutes and offered a prayer for the lost souls. Finally, with a long sigh, she stood up and gently ran her fingers over the name on the plaque. She made no attempt to hide her tears, slowly moving away from the plaque.

'You guys roam around for some time; I'm coming in ten minutes. I'm sorry for leaving you again, but I promise I'll be back in ten minutes this time.'

Leaving us, Tatiana headed for the pine forest on the hillside in front. I sat near the memorial plaque and closed my eyes. I tried to visualize the procession of boys and girls gathered here on that day.

Siddhartha looked at me and said, 'Just like lightning without clouds, the mortar shells of the Serbian army must have ripped apart the bodies of the boys and girls that day.'

Looking away, I saw Tatiana leaving the dark green pine forest behind and walking back with long strides. Siddhartha and I got back to the car. It looked like Tatiana had been crying.

I checked my watch; it was half past five.

Siddhartha said, 'I will sleep, so I am sitting in the back seat.'

'Would you like to sleep with your head on Tatiana's lap?

Shall I ask her to go to the back seat? After a few days, your wife is coming, is not it?' I asked in pure Bengali.

'Don't talk rubbish like an idiot. Rather Tatiana can sit in the front seat and give you company, since you are feeling lonely.'

'I already have enough good relation with her. Why shall I make further advancement?'

As Tatiana approached us, Siddhartha said, 'Tania, you sit in front, this nature lover will learn the botany chapter from you. I want to sleep a little.' Siddhartha quickly opened the back door and got in.

'Hey, what was the fight between you two? I am not so familiar with him!'

'That's what I want. Please gossip with him.'

Tatiana sat down next to me in the front, and we set off for Doboj. I stared at her face, glowing in the soft, fading sunlight. She was sitting quietly, so I thought to myself that if after leaving the city and taking the main road, she didn't speak or cried silently, then I would try to talk with her.

Tatiana took out a handkerchief from her vanity bag and dabbed her eyes. Thinking that it would be rude to look at her face directly, I kept my eyes on the road and accelerated away.

Was Tatiana's body shaking occasionally?

'Are you feeling unwell? Shall I stop the car for a while?' I asked softly.

'Nah, I'm fine, nothing to be worried about,' she replied.

I realized that everything wasn't right, as she started crying. She looked at me and said, 'I'm sorry, I can't help myself. You may be wondering how I became so emotional!' Tatiana whispered, looking straight at the road.

I looked at Tatiana in amazement. I said, 'Everyone has the right to be emotional, who can say who'll be emotional and when! I don't mind at all.'

This time, Tatiana said softly, 'My father was a bank officer, and I studied English literature at Tuzla University, One day, at the age of twenty-one, when I came to visit this Pannonia Lake during my vaction, I fell in love with Shali Imamovich. He was a twenty-three-year-old third-year student at Tuzla Medical College. We used to ride around on motorbikes in those places where I took you today. We used to go farther distances up to the hillock. He was addicted to mountain climbing. His father still owns a large fruit shop at Freedom Square, and one of his sisters, Shamima, is currently studing at medical college. On 25 May 1995, we came to this rally for Marshal Tito's birthday. Many of our friends had gathered at this park in Kapija around eight in the evening. Everyone was busy enjoying themselves when the shells were fired in the middle of the crowd, and it created a pandemonium. I fell unconscious at the sight of Shali's decapitated body. Next morning, I woke up in a hospital bed without a scratch on my body. His tormented eyes still haunt me when I am alone.'

'Oh my God! I had no idea.'

'I went to their house to meet his mother and sister. I took my lunch there. The real story is not known to the people of their house. On that day, after getting permission from the house, Shali wanted to ride his bike along the shore of the lake, which was secluded. On the other hand, I've always loved hustle and bustle, and it was I who took him to Kapija that day. So, I feel responsible for this tragedy. Whenever I get a chance, I repeatedly apologize to Shali with flowers at his grave; he smiles and looks at me. Even today, he is lying in absolute peace with the same smile, but my smile has been taken away forever.' Tatiana let out a loud sigh and fell silent.

I dropped Tatiana at an alley near the cinema hall when we reached Doboj at around seven in the evening. She dragged herself out of the car as if the burden of grief was too heavy for her body to carry.

Twenty-three

If you work more, it will exert a lot more pressure on you—this is the hard realization in my life. As a part of my next assignment, I was tasked with conducting the reconnaissance of several burnt villages.

For the Serb Army, it was not enough only to evict the villagers through brute violence and terrorism, but it was mandatory to induct fear in the minds of the villagers so that they would never think of returning to their native village. This is the principle of ethnic cleansing. News of mass graves came in almost every other day at the Doboj Regional Office, with many other villages like Polje, Vlasenica, Zvornik, Bosanski and Bradina already being excavated. Bosnia's civil war killed nearly 0.25 million people and left more than 0.50 million missing. Many of the two million people who had left never returned. Many people did not know where their beloved and relatives were. One time, I could see from a distance the natives returning to their villages—their heads hanging with the burden of grief. I saw fear in their eyes. I saw pain and helplessness writ large on their faces. Even after witnessing war, oppression, humiliation and death, these people had no complaints, as if they had accepted it as a mockery of their destiny. The UN and many other NGOs had been working tirelessly for the reconstruction of Bosnia.

One afternoon, Suzanne suddenly came to the office looking exhausted. She could secure a transfer for herself to the MHQ when she specially requested one to be closer to her brother, who was being tried in Sarajevo. She was staying with her beloved uncle, and spending all her time working at the MHQ and rushing to court every now and then.

After moving to Sarajevo, on several occasions, Suzanne had wanted to spend time with me, but I resisted. This time, I offered to spend some time with her.

'I will come one day definitely, you may rest assured, I will come to you,' she said, leaving just as suddenly as she had come.

∽

At the beginning of the second week of June, Siddhartha's wife and daughter arrived in Doboj, and a few days later, they left for a tour of Europe.

Because of my work, I became close to Abdullai Mamuni of Ghana and Marchin Kozulinski of Poland. At the end of the office hours, I spent time with them in shopping malls and roaming around small villages. Marchin was quite fond of the home-made local wine *rakija*, so I accompanied him to distant village bars on a few occasions. Marchin used to sit and drink in a bar, while Abdullai and I went around the village talking to the local villagers. They talked about everything—from work and love to daily grind, but when it came to the topic of war, they always went silent.

Meanwhile, Siddhartha returned from his Europe tour with his family. After a few days of busy and hectic shopping schedule, his wife and daughter left for Calcutta. Siddhartha also became a part of our touring team.

The four of us wandered around in new places until the second week of July, when Marchin's repatriation order came in and Abdullai was transferred to Bihach.

Abdullai hugged me as soon as I told him that I was coming to Bihach one day. He said, 'My countryman, Christopher has gone to Ghana on holiday. I have asked him to bring me elephant trunk. As soon as he returns, I will call you to relish soup made from elephant trunk.'

∽

I fled from Calcutta to escape the fatigue of monotonous work; however, it hadn't left me. One day, I came back tired from office and lay down on the bed when there was a knock on the door. I got out of bed and opened the door. Siddhartha entered like a storm. 'Are you still not ready? It is almost six o'clock. It will be dawn before we return from Banja Luka if we don't start now. Please get ready quickly.' When I showed no urgency, Siddhartha enquired, 'Do you have fever or something?'

'No, no, no fever, I am mentally exhausted.'

'Go freshen up and change your clothes. I am making tea for you.'

Siddhartha handed me a cup of hot tea as soon as I came out of the washroom.

I finished my tea and said, 'It's too late for a long-distance ride to Banja Luka today. Let's go somewhere nearby.'

We got into the car and were on the road to Sarajevo, with Rafi-Lata's duet playing on the tape, '*Teri duniya se door, chale hoke majbur, mujhe yaad rakhna.*' Siddhartha paused the music and looked at me, 'I haven't talked to my daughter for the last four days.'

'Why, couldn't you contact Calcutta?'

'The post-war telecommunications system has not improved here that much. The office said that the system was down due to some satellite problems.'

I understood why Siddhartha was upset.

'Are you going to Suzannes' house?'

'No, no, she's not in Prada now, she has moved to Sarajevo on deputation duty at the MHQ. Let's go to a good place nearby.

I will show you a place where Suzanne had taken me earlier.'

'So, that's the point! But would you like my company in such a special location?'

In the meanwhile, we left the asphalt road and advanced 2 kilometres further to a small place called Domaljevac. The river Bosna coiled here like the English letter 'S'. Two hills, about 400–500 feet high, on either side of the Bosna, stood like silent sentinels at the mouth of the coil.

It had rained during the first week of August. The most interesting thing was that anybody could drive down the river following the foothill trail. Siddhartha was overjoyed when we came down to the riverbed laden with beautiful pebbles while driving along the foothill.

There was a steep rise after the two hills, so the pebbles were beautifully smooth and well-shaped. The hills were bare, devoid of any big tree, but the whole valley was wrapped in a carpet of golden-green grass, with many colourful flowers sprouting in the bed of the grass. The most noticeable spectacle, however, was a small patch of grass sprinkled with myriad small red and yellow flowers. The shadow of a whole mountain was visible in the sparkling water of the river at this hour.

'Take off your shoes and socks, we are going down for a stroll into the stream today, you'll feel excellent walking barefoot on the pebbles,' I said.

'Why? Do you want to sing today? *"Chhappak chhai, chhai chhappa chhai, paniyo ke chhite udate hui"* I assume that you definitely went into the water sport with Suzanne here!'

'No, when I came with her, it was the first week of February. The river was frozen over.'

'I have to admit that the girl has a praise-worthy taste!'

'Yes, she had come here before me with her parents and brother. She told me she would come back with me at the end of next May!'

'So, that is the reason you have brought me here?'

'Suzanne is not available; therefore, you are the only person to accompany me!'

While walking on the pebbles, I stepped into the water. Just then, I noticed a medium-sized pale-white stone shining in the transparent water. It felt smooth under my feet. I dipped my hand in the water to retrieve it when I realized that it was not a stone but an unbroken human skull, a whole skull! There were still eight teeth in the upper jaw clearly visible.

Siddhartha also stepped into the water, 'What is that? I should also take a look at it! Oh, it must be the skull of someone who was killed during the genocide.'

I came up from the water with the skull in my hand. Examining the skull, Siddhartha said, 'It may be of a child or a girl.'

'The skull is always much smaller than the head. Apart from that, there is no lower jaw, so it looks comparatively smaller,' I said.

'The incident should be reported officially.'

'Look at the country! More than 0.25 million people were killed in the civil war and 0.5 million people are missing. Out of 4.5 million people, who would bother with a mere skull? No need to score this issue, if we had gotten a whole skeleton, we could have reported it.'

My perception of digging many mass graves had made me more reasonable, but at the same time, I was shocked by my own answer.

'You're a science student, you've studied physiology. You can guess whether it's the skull of a woman, a child or a man.'

'Rather we could give it a name, what do you suggest?'

'When we don't know whether it is of a woman or a man, how to give it a name?'

After much argument and contemplation, we came to

the conclusion that it was the skull of a young girl who was mercilessly murdered. If not so, then why should the head be left in the river so carelessly?

Out of many names suggested, we chose the name Yashminka.

Then we proceeded to pay our tribute to Yashminka. I washed and cleaned the sand and mud from the skull very carefully. In the meantime, Siddhartha brought a handful of wild flowers. Finding a groove in the middle of three large boulders at the foot of the hill, I placed Yashminka in the middle. With great reverence, I spread flowers on the skull, brought soil from the surroundings and made a grave for it. It was clear that she had been tortured. I also knew that there would never be a trial for the killing of this girl, but I felt we, as human beings, had done our duty.

∽

When I reached office the next day, Maria came to meet me. 'Please order for coffee. I saw that your papers were lying in the receipt section, so I brought it to you directly,' she said.

'It is the duty of Dragana to bring these correspondences to me, but I don't see her today. I should have gone and brought the papers from her table.'

'I went to the MHQ yesterday. I am here to share a secret with you. I heard that you are going to be appointed the regional commander in Tuzla. Don't tell anyone now, otherwise those who are aspiring will interfere and distract the decision.'

'Phew, I'm not interested at all. Moreover, I did not give the option, so how will they select me?'

'No, the MHQ won't do anything without your opinion. But why don't you want to go? It's a great opportunity. You will not get much money, but you may command over a region. It is quite satisfying. Moreover, you will have an advantage in the next missions. If you do a good job there, you can become a deputy chief in the last one or two months.'

'Oh no, there are so many problems in my country, so if I have to do policing, I will do it in my own country, and I will not come to the UN mission once again.'

'Why don't you like to work with the international community? You have friends from so many countries here, is it not worth it?'

'It sounds good, but our country also has a lot of opportunities to work, I want more job opportunities for my people.'

'Exactly, come to the point, that's what I was saying. If you were the regional commander, you would have agency and the sphere of work supervision would get bigger.'

'No, I want to work on Ground Zero.'

'Look, think twice about what you will do,' Maria got up after finishing her coffee.

I turned the letters over and saw that almost all of them were from the local people and one from Suzanne. I opened Suzanne's letter, written in large fonts, most probably with lipstick, 'Missing You - Suzanne,' that's all. Thinking about Suzanne's condition made me upset. Most of the complaint letters were usually forwarded to various IPTF stations for enquiries, but once in a while, I read some of the complaints. That was actually Dragana's job as most of these complaints were written in the local language.

I called Dragana. The phone kept ringing for a long time. Just as I was about to put down the receiver in annoyance, someone picked up the call and shouted into it, managing to say a few words before the line got disconnected. The girl was saying something in a local language. I came out of the chamber and found Tatiana in the corridor and asked for her help.

I called back on Dragana's phone again. This time, Tatiana was talking, she whispered a few times and ultimately disconnected the phone. She looked at me and said that there was some problem with Dragana's pregnancy. She had been admitted to the hospital, so she could not make it to office.

With a loud sigh, Tatiana said as she sat down in the chair, 'You probably don't know out she's been evicted from her house, there's no one with her in this crisis period except the nurse.'

'Okay, I'll go visit Dragana in the hospital, see if I can be of some help to her. Which hospital is she in?'

Twenty-four

Seeing me beside her bed, tears flowed from Dragana's eyes as she lay in the hospital cabin. I wiped her tears with the cotton on the table next to her and said, 'It's okay, don't worry about going to office, I'm by your side. You have your own principle and have taken a decision, let me say something, you will be the ultimate winner.'

'There will be no harm to my baby, no?'

'Let me speak to the doctor first.'

I came out of the cabin looking for the doctor.

As soon as the name Dragana was mentioned, the doctor said, 'She okay, *nema problema*.' The doctor said something more, but I could not understand a single word of it.

I came back, sat beside Dragana's bed and repeated what the doctor had said, '*Nema problema*.'

'Yes, he also told me that they'll release me from the hospital by tomorrow. I will come to the office after two days' rest.'

'Don't worry about coming to office. I'll tell Maria and we'll arrange for an LA for the time being. Take your own time. If you don't mind, I'll come to your flat every evening on my way back from office and see you.'

'It's my pleasure, you're always welcome.'

This time, Dragana was holding my hand, so I couldn't even get up if I tried to. She gave a pale smile and said softly, 'People who are so close to me, those whom I have loved so much since my childhood are not by my side today. But look, you are completely unknown to me. I have been working with you for only a couple of months. Your house is a few thousand kilometres away, but you came to see me. I am indebted to you forever. It's getting late, you should get back to office.'

I came back from the hospital and went straight to Maria's office, 'Please provide me with a temporary LA till Dragana recovers completely and can resume her duties.'

'I will assign Biliana Simich, she is my LA. And please think once again about the proposal from the MHQ for the new posting, it's my request.'

'Ok, I will rethink.'

Reaching up to the door, I came back, 'What else can I think? I've completed eight months already in the mission, and maybe four months on this assignment is left. I do not want to change my assigned responsibilities or place of duties. It's been a great experience working in the UN. I get a lot of money, but I can't disregard my country as well.'

Maria looked a little disappointed. I realized the MHQ had given her the responsibility to convince me so that they may send me to Tuzla.

'I am very much involved in the work here. I will not be able to finish these before the end of the mission. So, I am not willing to take on new responsibilities again,' I told her, hoping she would understand.

I came back to my chamber and sat down with Biliana, who read and translated the applications at hurricane speed. She looked at me through direct eye contact, put a smile on her face and said, 'If you have to translate anything else, tell me. I will do it.'

'Yeah! One prisoner from Teshlić correctional home complained that the jailor has put him under tremendous mental torture. He is not even provided with proper food. Please translate the complaint for me and endorse the other petitions to the respective stations.'

An hour before the end of office work on Saturday,

Siddhartha rushed into my chamber and said, 'Get up, get up, I'm going to take you to a new place today.'

'There is still a lot of work left, give me an hour.'

'No, no, then it will be too late, get up now, we will go to Banja Luka.'

'It's about half past five now. We have 200 kilometres to cover going and coming back. That too through hilly roads full of forests! There'll be a shortage of time to execute the programme.'

'Why? Are you scared?'

'No, I'm not afraid at all. I have heard that the road gets secluded from Prnjavor. So, I'm trying to be cautious. If some mishap occurs, I've to spend the whole night in a broken-down vehicle with a hefty macho boy!'

'Here we are, 5,000 kilometres away from home—is there any difference between Prnjavor and Doboj or any damn place?'

Running out of excuses, I shut down my computer and came out of the chamber.

'You change out of your uniform and put on your formal suit. I'm getting ready too.'

'What is this about a formal suit?'

'Hey! Banja Luka is the place of pure sahibs and memsahibs. Moreover, this is summer weekend. What is the problem if we go a little dressed up?' Siddhartha got out of the elevator and drove away.

∽

It was six o'clock when we started our journey.

Leaving Modriča Road on the right, I took a left turn and drove along Januwa Road to Banja Luka. I slowly climbed the hill, driving carefully along the zigzag road, with a Hemanta-Sandhya duet playing on the tape.

Siddhartha was very excited. 'Such a wonderful place! I came here via Maglaj on the way to Zenica once.'

While on the road, the red rays of the setting sun falling on the distant mountains created a strange enchanting atmosphere. Dense pine forest was spread along the road for the next few kilometres. The environment was quite thrilling, scary even.

We reached Prnjavor at seven in the evening. Siddhartha said, 'Stop the car. I am famished. I have heard that very good ćepavi is available here. We should eat here.'

I parked the car and waited by the road. Siddhartha came back after some enquiry. He was informed by the locals that up ahead the road there was a restaurant called Osaka, where we would find good ćepavi.

Osaka was a crowded place. A group of young male and female customers dressed in provocative clothes were sitting at a table. When the restaurant manager said something, a few of them made some space at a table for us. Boys and girls were smoking. The restaurant was filled with smoke. We didn't even try to sit down at the table and said, '*Fala, fala*, we are comfortable. *Emma parcella*, we're happy to take the parcel of ćepavi.'

The manager was annoyed and said something to the boys and girls. They grinned and ignored the manager's annoyance.

'This is the young generation,' Siddhartha noticed their behaviour. 'How easily they ignored the old man?'

The sun was still shining brightly when we set off for Banja Luka after having ćepavi and cappuccino.

We reached Banja Luka at half past nine in the evening. This city was the pride of Bosnian Serbs. Many important events of the civil war had taken place in this city. The NATO attack also started with this city. But today, Serbian young men and women dressed in trendy dresses roamed the streets. From dancing to playing the guitar and the saxophone, one could see so many sights on the streets.

Siddhartha said, 'These people know how to enjoy life!'

'Read the reverse page of life also,' I added.

'What is in the reverse page? Just see what is going on in the streets, in the discotheques, in the clubs, in the pubs. They are having pure and simple fun. None of them are hiding anything. They are not hypocrites like us. They do whatever they want in front of everyone.'

'Can it be a healthy life? They are behaving like drug addicts!'

'Okay, okay, stop, now I'm taking you to a place and let's see if you like it.' Siddhartha took the wheels and drove to the Banja Luka Cathedral. 'Don't get out of the car, only take a look at the place. I will bring you here another day. We will stay for a whole day. The architecture here is worth seeing.' After crossing the cathedral, Siddhartha drove along the road on the banks of the river Vrbas and entered the Hotel Jelena. He looked at the watch.

'Are you hungry again?' I asked.

'No, boss, I'm not hungry, but I guarantee you will like it here. You will not want to leave this place easily today.'

The hotel lobby and courtyard were decorated with brightly coloured lights, fine fabrics, etc. Sitting in the car, I understood that we had entered a wedding pavilion. A number of men and women dressed in gorgeous clothes were walking around the hotel premises. Before I could ask him anything, Siddhartha parked his car in the parking lot and said, 'Stay in the car I will be back in a short while.' Siddhartha came back five minutes later. 'Go through the lobby of the hotel to Room 18. It is on the second floor. Once you reach there, ring the bell. There is someone waiting to meet you there. That person will tell you what to do next. We have four hours. We'll try to get out at two in the morning. So, you can take your time. Best of luck, my boy!'

Before I could probe him further, Siddhartha disappeared into the crowd.

I didn't understand what he said. Before leaving, Siddhartha had asked me to wear a formal suit. Did he come to attend someone's wedding? I was a little annoyed. So, that was the excuse to come visit Banja Luka. I thought to myself. He had dragged me so far to attend the wedding of someone he knew well. He basically needed a driver-cum-companion. He could have clearly told me that.

Crossing the hotel lobby, I went upstairs to the second floor, went to Room 18 and pressed the bell with curiosity. A few seconds later, the door to the room opened. Surprisingly, my breath stopped, and for a moment, it seemed as if all the blood in my body had come up to my throat.

'Why are you standing there like a fool?' Suzanne grabbed my hand and pulled me inside the room and shut the door. She jumped up and hugged me tightly and kissed me on my lips. She whispered, 'I didn't expect you to come!' After an hour and a half, she said, 'Let's have dinner.'

When I met Siddhartha in the hall, he asked me with a mischievous smile, 'How was the surprise?'

'You could have told me before you left!'

'If I did so, would you have been this happy? I wanted to surprise you. It was all Miriana's plan. I don't deserve any credit.'

'Who is Miriana?'

'She was my LA in Zenica. It's her wedding today.'

'So, how did Suzanne come here?'

'Do you remember Hamza Hedich? He is the groom. You may recall, a few months ago, on the way back from Sarajevo, you drove to Zenica along with Suzanne. She left the IPTF station with a handsome guy. You were jealous. That macho man was Hamza. He is an aeronautical engineer working for Swiss Air.'

I shook my head and said, 'I remember, but you're wrong about me being jealous.'

'You are the best judge of what is right and wrong. But

the look on your face that day was telling. There was utter disappointment in your eyes.'

Suzanne said, 'Hamza is Suleiman's elder brother. When Zainab married my father, Suleiman was very young, so Zainab took him with her to our house. Later, my father adopted Suleiman. But Hamza stayed with his close relatives after his mother's remarriage.'

'What about Suleiman?' I asked.

'He got the bail three days ago and is now back home. He is here somewhere. It was worthwhile for me to go to Sarajevo,' Suzanne replied.

'Suleiman has no blood relation with you. He is not even your half-brother. What you did for Suleiman has no comparison, Suzanne!' I exclaimed.

'No, that's all we have to do as human beings. Moreover, we had done a great injustice to Zainab's family at one time. You don't know everything. Let's go upstairs for dinner first.'

We all had our dinner together. I had never seen a more stunning bride than Miriana, and whispered my feelings to Suzanne.

'Miriana is naturally very beautiful. Now that she is decked up in bridal attire, she looks like a fairy. Don't worry, I will look even better in a bridal dress,' Suzanne whispered looking at my eyes with a smile on her face.

After dinner, everyone gathered in the hotel lobby. I accompanied Suzanne and Siddhartha to the wedding ceremony. I was intently observing the familiar rituals. Suddenly, Suzanne pinched me.

'You need to go to washroom. So, why are you standing here like a fool?'

'Who told you that I have to go to washroom!'

'When you'll get married, you will be taught everything afresh. No need to memorize the hymns of other's marriage ceremony!' Suzanne answered rolling her eyes.

I realized that Suzanne was indicating me to go upstairs.

Without saying a word, I quietly stepped back from the crowd.

After a while, Suzanne entered the room. She turned her back towards me and said, 'Please take off this dress.' I slowly pulled the zip of her dress down, which revealed her beautiful back in the dim light. Sitting on the bed, she said to me, 'Pull the dress down, the frock is pressed close to my waist.' The dress came out as I pulled a little. Just as I was about to hug Suzanne, she pushed me away and said, 'Leave me, I'm perspiring like anything! Wait a minute please, I've to take a bath first.'

Twenty-five

Fifteen minutes later, Suzanne came out of the washroom totally naked. I couldn't take my eyes off her. She said, 'I know your friend has a meeting tomorrow at half past eight in the morning, but today I will not let you go. Early morning, you can take my car, and let your friend leave at night according to his plan.'

'He is a terrible driver. I cannot let him drive back alone such a long way.'

'Let him go to hell then. Why should I compromise?'

'Please don't be so harsh. My relationship with my friend will be jeopardized. I have promised him I'd go back by two. I can't reschedule now.'

'All right, you don't have to go. I'll call Suleiman, he'll arrange a room for your friend and let him know that you guys are leaving at five in the morning. It is a well-known fact that in the middle of the night "white ladies" roam the road of Prnjavor with their feet upwards! That'll help Suleiman convince your friend.'

Suzanne called Suleiman and explained the matter. She set her alarm to quarter to five, kept the phone down and said, 'I know I have to put up with a lot of comments in the morning, but now I am helpless and want your full attention!'

At midnight, I woke up in discomfort. Suzanne was lying on my chest, and I felt suffocated under her weight. I left the bed while gently moving her and went to the washroom. I saw Suzanne sitting on the bed when I came back.

She came back from the washroom and said, 'When Bosnia-Herzegovina planned to declare Independence in the late 1900s, my father served in the Serbian army and worked on a special assignment in Zenica. Serbian President Slobodan Milosevic and Commander Ratko Mladić didn't want Bosnia-Herzegovina's independence. An intel report from mid-December stated that a few big leaders of the Muslim terrorist groups were arriving in Zenica. The local Muslims considered them revolutionaries and freedom fighters. Most of the people branded terrorists or separatists by government, are, in fact, revolutionaries and freedom fighters.'

'You're right. In freedom movements, the antagonists are always peoples' heroes, but they are viewed as enemies by the ruling parties.'

'The Serbian army had already received the news that those heroes would be meeting at Zenica. My father led a team of Serbian soldiers to either capture or eliminate these terrorists. The meeting time was the evening of 24 December. My father and his team set up an ambush. In those days of the revolution, Saudi Arabia and some Middle-Eastern countries were funding some jihadist and the Bosnian Muslim freedom fighters. Leaders of several of those groups had been gathering since that afternoon. Zainab's husband, Belal Hedich, was on his way to the meeting house, which was cordoned off by my father's forces. One of my father's team members shot Belal dead, leading to the escape of all the gathered leaders, thus thwarting the army's plans to capture the revolutionaries.

'My father picked up Belal's body from the spot for identification, when Zainab arrived with her two young sons. She fell on the dead body and started crying.'

'Zainab, your stepmother, right?'

'Yes. My father admitted his mistake and took care of the family. Eventually, my father married Zainab and brought her to Prada along with the child, Suleiman. Later on, he adopted him, while his elder brother Hamza stayed on in Zenica with his relatives. Dad also took all the responsibility of his studies.'

'I believe your education in being a great human being stems from your father, as he was a great man himself. The state should have taken the responsibility for collateral damage; however, it was shouldered by your father.'

At five in the morning, I started for Doboj with a visibly annoyed Siddhartha. My resolution to not talk to him was because of my embarrassment from last night's issue. I concentrated on reaching early. Within the hour, we crossed Prnjavor.

Siddhartha, annoyed by my silence, asked, 'Are you not ashamed? Isn't this the place where "white ladies" roam on the road with their feet upwards during night? Did the *sada petni* (white ghost) tread on your bed last night or was she dancing like Maa Kali on your chest?' He continued, 'Is a tiger chasing us? Why are you driving at such a speed?'

'Your grumpy face doesn't look any better than a tiger's face, you know?'

'Oh, really?' Siddhartha shot back.

When we reached Doboj, Siddhartha got out of the car and disappeared.

∽

In mid-August, the temperature rose to about 30 degrees Celsius, which we, Calcuttans, were habituated to. However, for the Bosnians, the hot topic was the rise in the mercury levels. With the rise in temperature, the sahib and memsahibs of Bosnia finally shed their winter clothing, observing which Siddhartha commented, 'Let's buy some land, build houses and stay here!'

Like every other Indian officer on a summer tour of Europe, me and my team of ten officers from Kerala, Maharashtra and Delhi also did the same. In late August, we arrived in Switzerland via Croatia's capital Zagreb, after a two-day halt at Ljubljana, in Slovenia.

We first went to Lucerne, boating in the lap of nature, surrounded by the beauty of the magnificent Swiss Alps. After spending two days and a night, we arrived at Zurich. From there, we visited the important cities of France, Austria, Germany, Italy, Belgium and the Netherlands. During the end of September first week, we returned to Bosnia.

When I joined back work, I had piles of files waiting for me. I had to complete seventeen days of pending work in five days. The rainy weather continued through September.

Dragana was replaced by LA Juan Dafner, who became my friend within a few days. He invited me for home-made ćepavi and pita bread. We also took nature walks together.

∽

I received my transfer order for the post of deputy chief of human rights at the Sarajevo MHQ in the first week of October. Hearing this, Suzanne said, 'I also got a transfer to Doboj regional HQ. What does it mean? Perhaps, the Almighty does not want me to stay with you.'

Maybe that's our destiny!

After receiving the news from Suzanne, I felt disheartened.

Siddhartha said, 'Will you really go to Sarajevo? It's a matter of only two-and-a-half months, try to spend the time here only. Just get your transfer order cancelled.'

I also thought to myself that I would be back in Calcutta in the last week of December, and the promotion hardly offered any increase in salary. I went to Maria and said, 'You know everything, please arrange to cancel my transfer from here.'

Two days later, Maria came to my office, 'You don't have to go to Sarajevo anymore, but you have to stay there for a few days in December, for archiving.' I was relived and readily agreed.

One day, Siddhartha said, 'Let's go to Mostar. The Ottoman Turks first occupied Mostar after entering Bosnia and then extended their territory throughout Bosnia.'

I sent a request for five days' leave to the headquarters, and we started excitedly planning our trip.

Subrata Chakraborty, an officer from Tripura who had come with us on deputation, was posted at Mostar. Siddhartha called him over the phone and requested him to book a hotel near the Neretva riverside area for our stay.

Subrata was very happy to get the news of our arrival. He said, 'I have travelled all over Europe but couldn't see Mostar properly. Great news, sirs, let's go to Mostar together.'

Before our trip, Suzanne came down to Doboj and insisted on going to Mostar with us. I explained to her that a single woman travelling with three men would not be acceptable in a country like ours.

She was adamant, and I agreed to talk to Siddhartha about it.

'No, no. It would not look nice. What will Subrata think?' Siddhartha retorted.

Even though she was upset, I had to say no to Suzanne.

Within a couple of days, Subrata got back to us saying that as all the hotels along the Neretva River charged a lot, he had booked us two rooms on the second floor of an old woman's house, right next to Stari Most.

On that predetermined day in the first week of November after lunch, I we set off for Sarajevo in Siddhartha's colleague Nahid's car. From there, we would go to Mostar on our own arrangement.

As we were getting off work, I met German monitor Aaron Groll, who asked us curiously, 'Where are you going with these big suitcases?'

Siddhartha said, 'Nahid is going to drop us off at Sarajevo, from there we'll go to Mostar.'

'Oh, you're going to Mostar. Seeing the big suitcases, I thought you guys were going back to your home permanently.'

'By God, we'll stay there for five days, will we not take luggage sufficiently?' I said.

'You Indians change your clothes too often.'

I put my hand on Siddhartha's shoulder and said, 'Leave it, he is teasing us.'

I turned to Aaron and said, 'Will you go to Sarajevo? Want to see us off? If so, then Nahid will have company at the time of his return.'

'I would love to go.'

Seeing Siddhartha still murmuring, I said, 'Look how nice he is! Within a second, he agreed to travel 350 kilometres just so that he can see us off.'

'Maybe he has some marketing to do and is just in it for the free ride.'

'Would we agree if someone proposed something like this to us?'

Siddhartha accepted my argument, unable to find any suitable logic in his favour.

Twenty-six

Nahid pressed the brake very hard when we approached the highway on the outskirts of Doboj city.

I sat on the seat balancing my body and looked through the windscreen. A hefty cat quickly crossed the road. Siddhartha said, 'Bosnian cats are just like the ones in Calcutta. They think every vehicle passing the road is coming to crush them. We believe that bad things happen when cats cross our path.'

I looked at him and shook my head, 'There are so many superstitions in our country. Even today, we wish success of the politicians in elections, cricketers on the field or cure for the ailing by chanting mantras, lighting lamps and ringing bells.'

Nahid might have hurt his knee against the dashboard. With a slight sound of pain, he straightened up and said, '*Urdu ya English me bolenge to mujhe bhi kuch samajh aayega, Janab* (Sir, I could understand something if you would speak in Urdu or English)!'

I told Nahid about all these superstitions in our country. Nahid smiled and said, 'There are more superstitions in Pakistan—my native place. After all, we were the same country before Partition. This *jharfuk bujruki* is very common there too.'

Observing Aaron feeling left out, I asked Nahid in English, 'Nahid, when is your repatriation?'

'It will be in three phases from the second week of November to the twentieth, but I am in the last batch. Come to Islamabad, I invite you all cordially. The various preparations of lamb kebabs and bread are to die for, I swear!'

'Thanks, Nahid, for your invitation; however, average Indians would not allow me to leave until I had had dinner with them. I took a rain check by feigning physical discomfort. Naimu came up with me to my car and offered one or two pieces of fresh snake his wife had brought from Shanghai. Back at my apartment, I vomited four or five times that night. I was in Zenica for a few more days after that incident. Believe me, I didn't dare go in the vicinity of Feng's apartment, fearing the snakes lying in his fridge, waiting to be my dinner.'

The four of us laughed a lot and ultimately Aaron said, 'You really survived Feng and his awfully frightening dinner!'

In the meantime, we crossed Zenica. The river Bosna was clearly visible from the highway. Zenica lay on the west bank of the river; 90 per cent of the population was Muslim, and during the Bosnian conflict, Zenica was the main place for the Muslim freedom fghters. Siddhartha was looking at the city of Zenica with curiosity.

'Who are you remembering so intently? Is it Laila or Olivera? If you wish, we can go to the station and meet both of them!' quipped Nahid.

'No, brother, I'm thinking about the beautiful parks and the warm behaviour of the people here.'

'So, who is hotter? Laila or Olivera?' Nahid was persistent.

'Don't cut such nasty jokes. Listen to me, Laila was raped eleven times in a single day during the war. Isn't it very shocking? Even after that, she suffered a lot. The Yugoslav National Army soldiers shot her father and grandfather in front of her eyes, even though they were never involved in politics or patronized the revolution. Her father worked in the municipality and her grandfather in a bank. Despite all these hardships, the girl tries to be happy and talks to everyone. Above all, she is not full of hate for anyone.'

Whenever I participated in discussion related to war or politics, I felt uneasy and embarrassed. The four of us were think of visiting thousands of countries, but they don't dream of visiting Pakistan,' said Siddhartha.

Aaron said, 'We broke the Berlin Wall and merged East and West Germany to atone our old mistakes. Then, why don't you just do away with the Radcliffe Line? Have you ever wondered that the whole world laughs at your meaningless arguments? What percentage of your budget is spent on defence?'

Nahid said, 'Yes, the armies have been making thousands of attempts to glorify themselves from the very beginning to overwhelm the people of our country, but according to the National Survey, their name comes at the top as some of the most corrupt.'

Siddhartha said, 'In India, that is not true because in our country, the army has not got the taste of absolute power like the Pakistan Army. There are many educated people in our country in politics now, but still they are few in number. As long as the baton of politics will be in the hands of idiots, the proper development of the country will probably not happen. Our election is based on mutual hatred, mentality to suppress and the seizure of power by conjuring up the imaginary ghosts of the deadliest enemy country who is sitting in the neighbouring state to encroach on our sovereignty.'

'Mushibbat aur pareshani ka is daur par hum phanse huye hain (We are stuck with this problem),' Nahid expressed discomfort and dissatisfaction.

The town of Zenica was approaching. Siddhartha said in Urdu, 'Don't discuss politics and hatred between the two countries before this German lad, he'll make fun of it.'

'That's right!' said Nahid. 'I have a funny story about Zenica. Naimu Feng's wife came from Shanghai to Zenica in the second week of January. Minas, a Greek monitor, and I went to Sarajevo airport with Feng to receive his wife. Minas left after receiving Feng's wife, while I accompanied them to their apartment. They silently listening to Siddhartha.

'Ah! Why are you being so sentimental, boss?'

'Because I'm a human being!'

'Oh, is that true? Are you human too? When you are saying it yourself, we have nothing to doubt about.' All four of us laughed together.

Aaron asked, 'Was the violence that took place in your country in February also due to such ethnic reasons? If you have less police, then why did you come here leaving your own country behind? You should see the interest of your own country first, isn't it?'

Siddhartha said, 'The dearth of police was not the reason, Aaron. How can I explain that complicated issue to this German lad?'

I understood Siddhartha's anguish very well. His grievance was not against Aaron, in fact, he was overcome with grief and shame as an Indian.

To change the subject, I said, 'Nahid, are you not driving to slow now?'

Nahid increased the speed of the car instantly.

The sun was setting in the southwest when we parked our car and boarded a Mostar-bound UN bus from Sarajevo.

It was late in the evening when we got off the bus at the UN Mostar regional office. As the regional office was at the extreme end of the city, we did not have much opportunity to see the city on the way. As soon as we got off the bus, Subrata came forward extending his arms with a smile on his face, 'Come on, sir, welcome to Mostar!'

'My jaws were aching from speaking English all the time. I am speaking Bengali after so many days.' We realized that Subrata was very happy to meet us.

'Sabyasachi, can you explain why our jaws ache while speaking English throughout the day? You have read all about the human physiology, so you can tell us.'

'Actually, we do not speak English much in Calcutta. And here, the English we speak is more like the natives; we use our jaws, exercising the whole tongue, squeezing and chewing the round words as flat as possible and let them out almost from the throat, so the jaws hurt.'

'I love you so much for doing the wrong analyses so confidently,' Siddhartha said laughing.

'Let's hurry up, I'm very hungry,' I said.

Subrata took us to his car. We kept our luggage in the boot and got in. Subrata said, 'Sir, if you don't mind, I will sing a Bengali song within my limit.'

Siddhartha said encouragingly, 'Of course, let there be a bit of Rabindra Sangeet.'

Subrata and Siddhartha sang Rabindra Sangeet in unison. Both of them were very happy. After a while Siddhartha said, 'What happened, Sabyasachi? Why are you silent? I agree that you are a little hungry, but still, you could join the chorus.'

'No way! I remember my Gangtok trip quite clearly.'

'Why are you remembering Gangtok while travelling in such a beautiful place like Mostar?'

'We were going to Gangtok for excursions while studying at the university. Observing the beauty of the river Teesta I tried to sing a befitting Rabindra Sangeet. From the back seat, my classmate Sushmita said, "Please stop, stop, you *asur* (demon). We'll drop you at the next stop if you sing another line; sitting on the bank of the river Teesta you may continue singing like a fox to your heart's content!" Sushmita had said it jokingly, but that incident remained with me. During that North Bengal tour, lots of emotions swept me, but I didn't dare sing a song.'

'This was an utter insult to the fox community; the foxes always call to the tune, as far as I know! However, we'll get back on the topic of Sushmita later on!'

Within a few minutes, Subrata left the road and took a right turn and parked his car at the gate of a small house. He stopped the car and pointed to the second floor of the house and said, 'I have booked your rooms here. Everything has been arranged, just give the old lady my name and she will show you to your rooms. Freshen up, I will come back in an hour and a half and pick you up. We'll have dinner at my place. I have cooked mutton. And, sir, don't worry, the food will not be out of tune. I have mastered the method through trial and error in the last nine months. Going back home, my wife's pride as a good chef can be wrecked.'

As we rang the doorbell, an old lady came out from the house and greeted us.

After exchanging greetings with a smile, we climbed the stairs to the upper floor, crossed the room, opened the door and came out on the veranda. Stari Most was in front of us. The river below was dark, so it was not clear whether there was water or not.

Siddhartha came and stood behind me. He whispered, 'The bridge was built of stone in the sixteenth century by Heruddin of Mima at the behest of Emperor Suleiman the Magnificent. Just imagine what not the bridge has witnessed since then? We'll take a walk on the bridge after dinner. What do you say?'

'Yes, I will definitely go.'

'History says, the Yugoslav National Army had been bombing this area since 3 April 1992, but they did not demolish the bridge. Ultimately, Bosnian Croats destroyed the bridge on 9 November 1993. Elsewhere in Bosnia, Muslims and Croats fought together against the Serbs, but here, they fought amongst themselves. At that time, many houses and mosques built by the Ottoman Empire were destroyed. Fortunately, a number of countries, led by Italy, have come forward to reconstruct the bridge.'

When we reached Stari Most on foot after dinner, it was

half past ten. There was some traffic on the bridge, which was under construction. The construction company's board displayed the names of countries that had sent aid for the reconstruction work.

Mostar could be considered the warmest place in Bosnia. When all other places are covered with snow for about five months a year, Moster recorded only a few days of snow.

Subrata said, 'Sir, do you know the name of this place, Mostar, has come from the name of this bridge—Stari Most? It was the administrative city of the Ottoman Empire in the Herzegovina region. Although the Austro-Hungarian Empire occupied Mostar in 1817, the city returned to Bosnia in the aftermath of World War I.'

Siddhartha climbed the half-broken bridge and said, 'Come here, let's sit together for a while on the railing of the historical ruins.'

Sitting next to him and me, Subrata said, 'There is not much water in the river, but whatever remains is very clear.'

'The municipality here must be very active,' I said.

'No, sir, actually the people here are very civilized. They will not throw even a cigarette butt anywhere other than a garbage bin,' Subrata replied.

The three of us sat side by side and sang many songs, though all of them were out of tune. There was no Sushmita here to throw us off the bus. We were the singers and we were the listeners too; no one to say anything.

Exhausted, Siddhartha said, 'Let's go to bed, it is quarter past twelve. When we visit Mostar tomorrow, we will come here again.'

After a long journey, I was quick to fall asleep and woke up at around quarter to eight. Going to the next room, I knocked the door. Siddhartha answered, 'I got up at half past six and took my bath. I have asked the landlady to serve us breakfast at half past eight. Come on, get ready quickly.'

When I came back to my room and opened the door to the veranda, I was awestruck by the view of the city bathed in bright sunlight and green as far as the eye could see. The old houses in the town and those scattered in the hills looked right out of a postcard. For a moment, my mind was filled with joy.

Shortly after, Subrata also joined us for breakfast and we got to discussing the itinerary for the day. Subrata said, 'Before going around the city, we will first look at the two big waterfalls called Kravica on the Trebizat River and Schlakovach in the vicinity of Mostar. Then, we'll go on a tour of the city.'

After breakfast, we got into the car, looking forward to an eventful day exploring the city. Surprisingly, the roads there were not very wide, but it was very clean and there was a lot of vegetation on both sides of the road. I had seen many dams in the country and abroad, but I had never seen a dam so secluded and surrounded by such big trees. The three of us went down to the Grabovig Dam and sat on a big rock with our eyes closed for about twenty minutes, the sound of the gushing water soothing our nerves.

Subrata broke the silence, 'I have been here twice before. Once with officers from the US, Ireland, Denmark, France and a few other countries, and the other with a Jordanian and two Egyptian officers. Both times were different, but this time, my mind is filled with a strange sense of calm.'

Siddhartha said softly, 'This time, it feels good because we are two people with whom you can speak in Bengali. The case of Bengalis is different. Moreover, it is in your subconscious mind that you have to leave this beautiful country and all these beautiful places in a few days and you'll never come back to this place in your lifetime again.'

It was getting late so we left the dam premises. Subrata drove the car towards the orchards again.

Along the road, on both sides, were forests of apple, fig, pomegranate, orange groves and the occasional vineyards. It was about three o'clock by the time we returned to Mostar, crossing rows of thousands of unnamed trees. Subrata took us to a small restaurant, where we had burgers, French fries and Coca-Cola.

After lunch, Subrata said, 'Now get some rest, we'll go out again in the evening.'

'Why don't you can come with us to our rooms? You can rest there too.'

We got back to our apartment and ended up spending the whole afternoon planning our next day's trip to Split. We decided to visit Medjugorje, famous for the 'Queen of Peace' statue. From there, we decided to cross the border into Croatia to visit Split and Dubrovnik.

As evening descended, we stepped out for a while into the town to visit the markets and soak in the local scene. Subrata helped was pick gifts for our families back in India and we came back to our apartment after a quick dinner.

Twenty-seven

The next day, we left at seven in the morning and reached Međjugorje within forty minutes. The town was a famous catholic pilgrimage site, especially Apparition Hill, which was the site where Virgin Mary reportedly appeared as a vision to a bunch of teenagers. Since then, the town came to be associated with numerous stories of miracles.

After having lunch there, we left for Split at three o'clock. However, the Croatian police were not willing to let us cross the border. Indians were not permitted to enter Croatia without a visa, not even for a day. They said, 'Sorry, this is the policy matter of our country!' We couldn't do anything after learning of Croatia's hatred towards Indians because of a rumour that India lent a hand to the Serbs during the Croatian Independence War. Disappointed, we went back to Mostar.

Before retiring for the night, Siddhartha came to my room and said 'We'll see tomorrow morning; moreover, we have to talk to Subrata before taking any concrete decision. Maybe there are some better places around.'

I fell asleep worrying about the plans for the next day.

In the morning, Siddhartha asked, 'Subrata, are there any mass graves here?'

'Why not? There are lots of mass graves at different places on the banks of the river Neretva and around the dams. But why do you want to see the graves here, haven't you seen enough already? Let me take you to the orchards we saw the other day.'

'Bosnia is on its way to become the world's biggest disgrace in the twenty-first century if they do not learn from their mistakes.

Okay, let's do a quick tour of the orchards and then, I was thinking, we could start for Doboj today.'

After breakfast, we loaded our bags in our car and went to the orchards on the west side of the city. Subrata was kind enough to pack some lunch for us, so we had a picnic there, after which we left for Doboj directly.

༄

I was surprised to run into Mazoor Hossain Changhaji when I was about to enter my apartment at around midnight.

Manzoor came forward after seeing me, '*Zindagi dhundhte dhundhte mout ke kareeb aa gaye hum, aur pyaar dhundhte dhundhte, Doboj paunch gayi woh kamsin kali* (While looking for I came close to death, and she reached Doboj looking for love)!' That was absolutely Brand Manzoor; whenever he would meet, there would be some sher-shayeri in pure Urdu!

'She has rented an apartment on the third floor of your building. Modriča station has been closed day before yesterday. The curtain is closing on the UN Mission. Most of the officers on deputation from foreign countries are returning home. With the exception of a few officers, almost everyone will be back in the third week of November. The European Union is taking over the responsibility of reconstruction of Bosnia from the UN. As UNMIBH will end in December, there is urgency of pack-up and rush to return home.'

'Who are you talking about, Manzoor bhai?'

'You didn't get it? I am talking about Suzanne. She's here finally. And she's been eating my head asking about you.'

Hearing Suzanne's name got my heart pumping. I composed myself and retired for the night, even though I wanted to go meet Suzanne immediately.

The next morning, I woke up late and hurriedly made it

to my office, where Suzanne was already waiting for me. She hugged me passionately and asked, 'Did you come back late last night or this morning? I was looking to surprise you by arriving suddenly at Doboj. I have arranged my posting here by asking Maria. Your Dragana will have her baby at the hospital. What do you say? Does the child really belong to her husband Joban or someone else?'

I was taken aback by the question. 'Dragana is a very faithful wife!'

'Oops, then why did Joban move away from her?

We had so much to talk about, but we checked ourselves because we were in office, and I had a lot of work pending from the days I had been away from Doboj.

About an hour later, Suzanne again rushed into my office with a big bundle of papers and said, 'You never had so much work pending previously?'

'After Dragana, Juan Dafner joined my unit. With him in Russia for a few days, I couldn't work properly.'

'Luckily, I got my posting here, as Modriča station is closed. I'll finish all your translations in the next three days anyway, but you have to take me to Disc Roma next Saturday and offer a good dinner.'

'Okay, I'll go with you for dinner, but you know I can't dance.'

'We will see to it in due course,' she said with a mischievous smile.

Suzanne called someone and said in fluent English, 'Thank you very much, I have got the flat key and I am leaving your apartment from today.' She slipped her hand into my pocket, took out my key and walked down the corridor.

'I'm going to keep my belongings in your flat. The rented flat upstairs belongs to an American. When I heard about your visit to Mostar for two days, I temporarily kept my stuff there.'

When we got back to work in full steam, I asked Maria for additional manpower to cope with the sea of complaints. Suzanne was also under a lot of pressure. If there were so many complaints, then why shouldn't the UN run the mission? I thought to myself. The stations of Modriča, Teslić, Zavidovići, Orašje, Vukosavlje and Zenica—all were closed, one by one, within two weeks. So, all the complaints were dumped on our regional office directly.

Around this time, came winter. The streets, parks, fields and riverbanks were filled with half-dried yellow leaves. Sixteen officers were being repatriated on 28 November, including Siddhartha.

When Siddhartha left, sensing my distress, Suzanne said, 'Don't worry. I'll take you to a new place every day so that you don't miss your friend.'

In the meanwhile, it was so comforting to have Suzanne live with me. We would stay up all night talking to each other. She narrated many stories of the inhuman atrocities—murders, rapes, lootings and arsons—committed during the war.

One night, Suzanne hugged and asked, 'Do you love me?'

'Why, do you have any doubts?'

'Then why aren't you marrying me?'

'I'm always ready. But you said that there are many issues that haven't been resolved yet, along with Suleiman's case and your master's degree.'

'I'm thinking of Suleiman's case; if we become less attentive now, he may face punishment. I hope the case is settled by March. I have decided to do my master's from India. So, I'm thinking, we could get married next spring.'

'Okay, as you are ready to be settled in India, I will come from Calcutta within fifteen days to pick you up. And for your master's, I will admit you to Jadavpur University; you will puff your golden tuft of hair and lead the tempest of revolution there.'

'Okay, I'm happy now.'

Twenty-eight

It started to snow in the first week of December. I didn't mind the cold anymore, as I had become accustomed to the chilly winter. Meanwhile, the new EU started coming in. We, too, began winding up our work at the UN.

On 15 December, Suzanne came to me and told that I had to write an efficiency certificate in her favour. She would then be able to appear in interviews in EU missions, at least till her brother's case was resolved. I really wanted her to find a suitable job. When I heard that my friend Andre O'Neil from Italy would be on the interview board, I made a phone call to him. I reassured Suzanne, 'You are more competent than the other LAs, so you shouldn't have a hard time getting a job in the EU even without a recommendation.'

Suzanne hugged me when I came to office after three days and informed me that she was joining the Banja Luka office from 20 December.

'I'm so sorry I can't stay with you until your last day,' she said.

'What else can be done, Suzanne? Your job is important.'

'Yes, I have to be patient and keep fighting for Suleiman until we have the final verdict in March.'

'Don't worry, spring is not far away, and we're getting married in April, so it's better to stay apart a little longer. I'll come with you to Banja Luka tomorrow.'

'Really?'

'Why not? I can't let you go alone.'

The next day, I was buried neck deep in work when Maria

came into my office and said, 'Make a dossier and prepare your work list. It will be handed over to the EU. Tomorrow, present your papers at Sarajevo and wait there to receive your repatriation order.'

Suzanne and I left Doboj at half past six in the evening and reached the Banja Luka hotel at half past ten.

'No, no, I will not let you go today. You Indians are not habituated and will never be able to drive on this slippery road so late at night.'

'Do you remember our first day in Modriča, Suzanne? How afraid I was driving? But now, I am quite confident. And the mission chief has told me to report at the Sarajevo MHQ tomorrow.'

'I understand, but you are not going today. Just wait a minute, I'm coming right now,' she said, running towards the hotel.

After five minutes, Suzanne returned with a polythene packet in her hand. She opened the door of the car and put the packet in the back seat, saying, 'These are some burgers and Coke for the road. Please drive carefully. Go, since you are determined, leave as early as possible.'

I noticed that she was crying, even though, she tried to hide her face with her hair. So, I parked the car and went after her.

When I caught up with her in the hotel lobby, Suzanne just hugged me, with tears rolling down her eyes. She whispered, 'I can't live without you. I have a dream of a very small world—just you and me!' I have come to know from the personnel section that your repatriation is on 24 December, I will come to see you off.'

'Yes, please do come that day. I will return to Bosnia as soon as Suleiman's case is resolved to take you back with me.'

'I am also sorting out all property matters back in Prada, but half of the house will remain in my name. My parents' graves are here, so I have to come back from time to time. I will quit my job as soon as you arrive in Bosnia in April.'

'Goodbye, my dear, I will call you as soon as I reach Doboj.'

ᗡ

I arrived in Doboj at four in the morning and called Suzanne immediately, 'I have just arrived, please go to sleep now.'

I fell asleep thinking about Suzanne.

The next day, I sat down to sort out all the paperwork before leaving for Sarajevo. While I was thinking of meeting Maria, she herself came down to bid me goodbye.

'I was just going upstairs to meet you,' I said.

'I didn't want you to get late, so I came down myself.' She handed me a small packet and said, 'By the way, your repatriation is on 24 December.'

When I returned to my hotel room in Sarajevo on 22 December around seven in the evening, I found Suzanne waiting outside my hotel room. She took the files from my hand and said, 'Open the door, there is something I need to discuss with you urgently.'

'All okay, Suzanne?'

'Open the door please, I will have dinner here tonight.'

'What is the matter?'

'I will tell you, but first, will you give me a tracksuit and a t-shirt? I want to change.'

I felt reassured seeing her calm down a bit and handed her a tracksuit and a T-shirt.

Suzanne entered the washroom humming a tune. After ten minutes, she came back from the washroom. Not only did she change, she also washed her hands and face. She looked out of the window and said, 'Remove the curtain, look at the heavy snowfall outside.'

I went ahead and removed the curtain, and in the light of a halogen lamp outside, I saw a heavy snowfall. Suzanne came to the window and stood beside me. The sweet fragrance of her body had an invigorating effect on me. I moved away from the window and asked, 'Now tell me what do you want for dinner?'

'Do you have any potato chips or just some tea?'

'I don't want any milk in my tea.'

'No, I also take tea without milk now.'

'Good habit, maintain it,' Suzanne said.

I came back from the small pantry with two cups of tea. Handing one to Suzanne, I sat down next to her on the bed. 'Now, tell me what important matter you have come to discuss?' I asked.

'It bothers me that you will leave this country the day after tomorrow,' she said, slightly annoyed.

'There is no alternative, Suzanne, you know that very well.'

Suzanne was sitting quietly.

'Tell me what happened?'

Just then she hugged me, and I realized that the thought of my departure was hurting her. I kissed her gently. Suzanne's body was shaking with emotion.

After a while, she looked at me and said, 'Will you take me with you to India the day after tomorrow? I'll be back in fifteen days, I promise!'

'How is that possible?'

'Why not?'

How could I explain to the girl that it was not possible to get her visa to India within a day? Moreover, she had just taken up a new job.

'I don't know, that you manage. What if you go to India and forget all about me? What if you go to Saira Banu in your country? So, I will go there and see everything with my own eyes and will come back again.'

'Saira Banu is my mother's age, and why are you talking about forgetting you?'

I went and stood by the window.

Suzanne came up to me and dropped her clothes, 'Look, don't you like me?'

'Why are you insulting yourself? Who else in the world is more beautiful than you, Suzanne? I like you very much. If you had told me about your decision even a few days ago, it might have been possible for me to take you to India. My departure is scheduled the day after tomorrow, you tell me how is it possible to take you along with me?'

'Then you stay here.'

'That is also not possible now. I have to surrender my diplomatic passport this time, and next time, I have to come back here with my ordinary passport. If you love me so much, just be patient for a few more months. I will come back and take you to India myself.'

'You promise?'

'I promise.'

Twenty-nine

At four in the morning, Suzanne drove out to Banja Luka for an important meeting. Before leaving, she said, 'In two months, I will come to India. I will have to return for Suleiman's case in March. Suleiman was my father's responsibility and now it is my duty to fulfil the commitment.'

I nodded in agreement. I went downstairs to say goodbye to her and came back to bed and fell asleep.

The next day, I woke up to a call from the reception. Although I couldn't understand all of it, I gathered that there was someone who wanted to talk to me. Taking half a chance, I said, 'Yes, I want to take the call.' I heard Suleiman's voice on the other end. He informed me that Suzanne had been shot twice in the shoulder and abdomen, and had been taken to Sarajevo's Dr Abdullah Nakas General Hospital.

My ears were buzzing, the room was spinning and it felt like there was an earthquake in my chest. I left the receiver and sat down on the bed, numb. After some time, I came out of the hotel room and asked the receptionist for directions to the Dr Abdullah Nakas General Hospital.

Arriving at the hospital, I rushed to the ICU on the fourth floor, and found Suleiman waiting there. He came forward and hugged me and said, 'Sorry, Sabyasachi, for disturbing you. She was calling out your name, even in a state of unconsciousness. One bullet hit her in the shoulder and broke the collar bone, the other one went inside her stomach and proved fatal; it is stuck in the liver, which is bleeding profusely. The surgeon has been informed and operation will be carried out as soon as he arrives.'

A nurse came out from inside the ICU and asked me, 'Who are you?'

'I'm Sabyasachi, the patient was murmuring my name,' I said.

The nurse took me by the hand and led me inside. Suzanne was lying on the bed with her head slightly raised. Her eyelids were closed, and her pale white face had an oxygen mask attached to it. I gently put my hand on her's. The eyelids trembled a few times—the same eyelids I had kissed so many times, which now had become swollen with visible veins.

'Look, Suzanne, I'm here.'

Suzanne opened her eyes slowly at the sound of my voice. Those expressive blue-brown eyes had disappeared completely, they were red now. Suzanne tried to look at me, but tears rolled down them. I took a handkerchief from my pocket and went to wipe her eyes. The nurse instantly objected, 'I will do that.' I saw her lips tremble. I put a little pressure on her hand. In a low voice, she said very clearly, '*Volim te*, I love you.' Then, completely exhausted, Suzanne closed her eyes.

'You are absolutely fine, get well soon, I will take you to India,' I whispered.

The nurse looked at me and requested, 'Mister, now you may go out of this cabin.'

As soon as Suleiman came out, he approached me and said in broken English, 'Suzanne was returning to Banja Luka. At five o'clock in the morning, when she reached Visoko, three young men stopped her car, their hands were in their pockets. They had big rucksacks on their shoulders. Suzanne thought they were asking for a lift. One of the three opened the door of the car, entered and shot her three times at point-blank range. The first bullet hit her on the shoulder and she immediately fell on the seat of the car. Then, the assassin shot Suzanne in the stomach. A third bullet hit the left window. Suzanne had a pistol on her, which she pulled out and fired back twice in a row, injuring probably one of them. That injured assassin was grabbed by the other two and they fled down the sidewalk.

'Could Suzanne describe this incident in her own words?'

'No, she fell unconscious in the car seat after firing. Abdel Zebbar, a Zenica businessman, was behind her car and saw the whole thing happen right before his eyes. He brought my sister to this hospital and called me from her phone.'

'Did Abdel meet you here?'

'Yeah, he was here until the police accompanied him to the station for registering his statement of fact.'

I couldn't believe Suzanne had any enemies or the fact that she carried a firearm in her handbag. I asked Suleiman, 'Who could be Suzanne's enemy? Do you know anything about that? Did you know that she has a pistol in her bag?'

'She was courageous and desperate but sometimes panicked. I think this pistol belonged to her father.'

'The day her father was killed, the assassins snatched one of his pistols, but there was another pistol in the house, I heard that from my mother.'

'Was it a terrorist group or a personal enmity?'

'I have no clue.'

Suleiman couldn't look directly into my eyes and I had a distinct feeling that he could be lying.

I was brainstorming to find a connection between Suzanne's shooting and Suleiman's case. Lately, Suzanne was too anxious to move to India with me.

I looked at Suleiman and asked, 'Are you sure that the pistol that Suzanne used was her father's?'

'Not sure, my mother said that the pistol was with Suzanne.'

'You must recognize it now.'

'It was not found in the car. One of the assassins took Suzanne's bag, the pistol and some other items from inside the car. Zebbar could not say exactly what they had taken.'

I stared at Suleiman with tear-filled eyes as my world came crumbling down around me. I learned from the MHQ that the day before yesterday the Zenica-Visoko region had been declared a Orange Zone for some time.

Suzanne's X-ray report revealed that a bullet was stuck in the left lobe of her liver and had to be operated on as soon as possible. She was bleeding profusely. Doctors here were waiting for the surgeon, Stephen Petrovic of the Sarajevo University Clinic.

Shortly after, Suzanne's uncle Ethan arrived with his wife in the waiting room. He recognized me at a glance. Coming forward, he put his hand on my shoulder and reassured me. Tears were flowing from Suzanne's aunt's eyes. I noticed her uncle's gloomy eyes turn blurred too.

Each moment spent waiting seemed too long and miserable. When news came in that Surgeon Petrovic had left his residence and was arriving within ten minutes, Suzanne was taken to the operation theatre.

When the surgeon came in, I rushed to him and before I could say anything, he said in clear English, 'I am not God. It will take a lot of effort to take out the bullet from where it is stuck. I will try my best, but pray to God so that I may be successful!'

We were all waiting for the operation to be over, but it was taking a lot of time, given how complicated the procedure was. After some time, Suleiman got up to leave the waiting room. I followed him to the cafeteria. Sitting with a coffee on a table in the corner, I observed him talking on the mobile for about three minutes. Then, he walked on the sidewalk in long strides with his hands in his jacket pocket, his head bowed down. I brusquely crossed the road to the sidewalk on the opposite side so as to not be caught by him.

After walking for about half a kilometre, he went into a house. Curious, I ran to the house and peeped inside through an open door. Suleiman was standing for prayers. I turned my eyes to the outside of the hall, it was not clearly visible from the outside, but I noticed that the house was a mosque.

I returned to the hospital. Every moment seemed to be dragged out. Three hours later, the surgeon came out of the operation theatre. Those of us who were waiting in the waiting room silently walked up to the doctor for an update.

'We had to remove one-fourth of the liver, as it was damaged by the bullets. Bleeding has stopped now, but we will have to wait until she regains consciousness to recover from the trauma of the impact of eliminating so much of her liver. She is still critical. I'm also very eager to see good results, next three days are very crucial.' Just then the hospital staff were taking Suzanne to the ICU in a trolley. I hurried a few steps forward and closely observed Suzanne.

Seeing the expressionless face, a shiver went up my spine. I closed my eyes. The only question in my mind was, 'Will Suzanne return from this situation?'

I didn't know when I had gone to sleep while waiting for Suzanne to regain consciousness. Suddenly, someone tapped my shoulder. I saw Maria standing silently behind me, with the chief of Human Rights and two police officers from the local police station. Maria pointed her finger at the local police officers and said, 'They want to talk to you.'

'Of course, it's my duty,' I looked at them and said, 'Yes, I'm ready.'

I earnestly requested them to allow me to stay in Bosnia for at least another seventy-two hours, until Suzanne's recovery.

'Why only seventy-two hours? You can stay for seventy-two years, but at present, you've to go to your country and report back there. I wish we could do something. As per your repatriation schedule, you have to leave this country by tomorrow,' said the chief of Human Rights.

Maria put her hand on my shoulder and said, 'We're mere players. If Suzanne's time is up, you can't prevent that. You have to go back to your country tomorrow. But the UN will be here to look into it. Your continued and energetic effort to find the truth will remain in the history of Bosnia, like a small dot.'

Mentally disturbed, I proceeded with the local police officers without answering.

I went to an empty room of the hospital and described everything I knew about Suzanne from the first day of the conversation.

After they left, I came out of the room and received the news that Suzanne had come to her senses a while back and had enquired about me. She was murmuring that she would also go to India as the atmosphere had become polluted and poisonous in Bosnia. I peeked through the glass door outside the ICU, but there was no way to see Suzanne's face. I was not allowed to enter according to hospital protocol.

It was dark when I arrived at the MHQ. I finished all my paperwork till the early hours of the next day.

When I reached the hotel at almost dawn, I saw Suleiman waiting in the lobby. 'Suzanne is in the same condition. She is in and out of consciousness. The doctor said that she is very critical, there is no improvement to mention yet.'

'I will be back in two or three days. For the time being, all the responsibilities are yours.'

Suleiman shook his head and left the hotel.

At eight o'clock in the morning, after handing over my vehicle at the MHQ and getting a clearance from personnel section, I left for the airport. While in the taxi, the city was diminishing, one village after another.

Will I really be able to come to this country one day? I thought to myself.

Just before going up to the boarding gate, I looked one last time at the arrival gate with my eyes filled with tears, hoping Suzanne would run through it just then. But alas, I was leaving her just when she needed me the most.

As the aircraft flew through the clouds, I imagined Suzanne standing in the white snow, waving her hand. Her voice is still ringing in my ears, 'I love you—*volim te, volim te...*'